Fragments of Tomorrow

OrangeBooks Publication

1st Floor, Rajhans Arcade, Mall Road, Kohka, Bhilai, Chhattisgarh 490020
Website: **www.orangebooks.in**

© Copyright, 2025, Author

All rights reserved. No part of this book may be reproduced, stored in a retrieval system, or transmitted, in any form by any means, electronic, mechanical, magnetic, optical, chemical, manual, photocopying, recording or otherwise, without the prior written consent of its writer.

First Edition, 2025

ISBN: 978-93-6554-099-4

FRAGMENTS OF TOMORROW

DR. SANJAY SINGH

OrangeBooks Publication
www.orangebooks.in

Foreword

In a world where screens whisper promises and cities pulse with the hum of tomorrow, *Fragments of Tomorrow* dares you to look beyond the noise. Ray Carter's story begins where so many of us have stood—on the edge of doubt, staring into a future that feels both infinite and suffocating. But this isn't just a tale of one man's fight; it's a mirror held up to our own lives, reflecting the power we wield with every thought, every choice.

Set against a 2042 skyline of neural implants and shimmering holograms, this novel weaves science fiction with a truth as old as time: reality bends to what we believe. Ray's journey—from a lost soul to a creator of worlds—challenges us to question the scripts we've accepted, the limits we've drawn, and the shadows that watch from the corners. With Leila's fire and Elias's wisdom lighting his path, he discovers that the greatest rebellion isn't against the world outside, but the one within.

For readers aged 16 to 30, this is more than a story—it's a call. To dream louder, to defy louder, to shape a tomorrow that's yours alone. *Fragments of Tomorrow* doesn't just ask what the future holds; it hands you the key and dares you to unlock it. Step into Ray's world, and you might just find your own.

Prologue
The Architect of Shadows

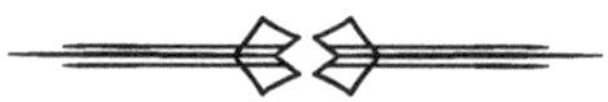

"The world is a mirror, forever reflecting what you choose to see."

— Unknown

The café sat nestled in a forgotten corner of the city, its chipped wooden façade a defiant relic against the relentless march of 2042's gleaming techscape. Holographic billboards flickered outside, their tailored ads whispering to passersby through neural-linked implants—*Upgrade your life! Only 999 credits!* —but within these walls, time seemed to pause. The air smelled of roasted beans and aged paper, a sanctuary stitched together by the soft clatter of mugs and the rustle of pages turned by hands that still preferred the tangible to the virtual. Elias sat alone in the corner, his silver hair catching the late afternoon light streaming through a cracked window, casting faint shadows across the open notebook before him. His weathered hands moved with deliberate grace, the pen carving ink into paper as if each word were a seed planted for a harvest he might never see.

The mind is a universe unto itself, he wrote, *a vast expanse where realities are born and shattered. What you believe, you create. What you fear, you summon. Most wander through life blind to this truth, reacting to shadows they mistake for substance. But there are those who see—those who dare to choose. And for them, the dance begins.* He paused, his sharp grey eyes lifting to scan the room. The barista rinsed a cup behind the counter, her movements mechanical, her neural implant glowing faintly at her temple. A couple murmured over coffee two tables away, their words lost to the hum of a drone hovering outside with a delivery. It was ordinary, predictable—a snapshot of a world most accepted without question. But Elias knew better. Beneath the surface, beneath the routines and the noise, something watched.

He'd felt it for years now—a presence, subtle but persistent, threading through the fabric of reality like a seamstress's needle. It wasn't God, not in any spiritual sense he'd ever chased in his youth. No, this was colder, more calculated. A framework, he called it in his quieter moments—a structure holding the world together, keeping it predictable, keeping it *contained*. He'd seen its edges in his own life: moments when choices he'd made seemed to ripple too far, when doors he'd opened slammed shut with no explanation, when shadows moved where no light should cast them. He'd spent decades piecing it together, testing its limits, and now, as his years dwindled, he knew he couldn't fight it alone. The notebook was his map, his legacy—a guide for those who'd come after, those who'd see what he'd seen and push further than he ever could.

The air shifted, a faint ripple brushing against his senses like a breath on the back of his neck. Elias didn't flinch. He'd grown accustomed to these disturbances, these whispers of the framework tightening its grip. He set his pen down, his posture stiffening as the café door swung open with a jarring chime that cut through the ambient hum. A young woman burst in, her breath ragged, her dark hair tangled as if she'd run through a gale. She wore a heavy coat despite the mild evening, its edges clutched tight in trembling hands. Her eyes—wide, frantic—swept the room until they locked onto Elias, a flicker of recognition sparking within them.

"Elias," she gasped, her voice barely above a whisper as she stumbled toward his table. "This was never supposed to happen."

He rose halfway, his expression unreadable but his gaze piercing. "Aisha," he said, her name a quiet anchor in the storm she carried. "What's wrong?"

She didn't sit. She leaned over the table, her hands gripping its edge as if it were the only thing keeping her upright. "They found me," she said, words tumbling out like spilled coins scattering across the floor. "I thought I could hide—thought I could keep it buried—but they know. They *see* me now."

Elias's jaw tightened, a shadow crossing his weathered face. "Slow down. Who found you?"

Aisha's eyes darted to the window, her breath hitching as if she expected the glass to shatter inward. "The suits. The ones you warned me about. They came last night—two of them, standing outside my apartment. They didn't knock. They didn't speak. They just… watched. And then—" She faltered, her voice cracking. "I woke up somewhere else—somewhere wrong. A room with no doors, mirrors everywhere, and my reflection—" She shuddered, wrapping her arms around herself. "It wasn't me. It was older, broken, staring back like it knew something I didn't."

Elias exhaled slowly, the sound heavy with resignation and resolve. He gestured for her to sit, but she shook her head, pacing a tight circle beside the table. "I can't stay still," she said, her voice rising with each step. "Not now. Not when they're this close."

"They've been close before," Elias replied, his tone calm but edged with steel. "You're still here."

"Barely!" Aisha snapped, then caught herself, lowering her voice as the barista glanced their way. "You don't get it. I've been careful—followed every rule you taught me. Focus on what I want, not what I fear. Don't react to the chaos. Shape the outcome. But last night, I woke up in that room, and it felt like they were pulling at my thoughts, unraveling everything I've built. I saw my life—my real life—slipping away, replaced by something I didn't choose."

Elias's eyes narrowed, a flicker of unease breaking his composure. "They're testing you," he said, his voice dropping to a near-whisper. "Pushing the boundaries of what you believe."

"Testing me?" Aisha's laugh was sharp, brittle, slicing through the café's quiet. "It felt like they were erasing me. Like everything I've done—the choices, the life I've made—it's slipping away."

He leaned forward, his hands folding together on the table, steady despite the tremor of age. "Listen to me, Aisha. They can't erase what you don't let them touch. Your mind is your fortress. They only win if you react— if you give them the power to define you."

She stopped pacing, her breaths shallow but steadying. "And if I can't stop them?"

"You can," Elias said, his certainty cutting through her doubt like a blade through fog. "You've already proven it. You're here, aren't you? You chose to find me instead of running aimlessly. That's strength. That's control."

Aisha sank into the chair across from him, her hands still trembling but her gaze sharpening. "You make it sound so simple," she muttered, brushing a strand of hair from her face. "Like it's just a matter of willpower."

"It's not simple," Elias admitted, a faint smile tugging at his lips. "It's the hardest thing you'll ever do. But it's the only thing that matters. They're watching because you're waking up—because you're starting to see the framework they've built around us."

"Framework?" Aisha echoed, frowning as she leaned closer. "You mean reality?"

"Part of it," Elias said, tapping the notebook with a weathered finger. "A version of it, anyway. One they've shaped to keep us blind, predictable. Most never notice. They live their lives reacting—anger to anger, fear to fear—never realizing they're handing over the reins. But you—you're different. You're a crack in their design."

Aisha stared at him, the weight of his words sinking in like stones dropping into still water. She'd known Elias for years, ever since she'd stumbled into this café as a teenager, lost in a haze of grief after her brother vanished without a trace. Elias had been there then, too, with his cryptic wisdom and unshakable calm. He'd taught her to focus, to choose her thoughts like weapons against despair. She'd built a life from those lessons—small but hers, a quiet defiance against a world that tried to dictate her path. But now, that life felt fragile, teetering on the edge of something she couldn't name.

"What happens to cracks?" she asked, her voice barely audible, her fingers tightening around the edge of her coat.

Elias's smile faded, his eyes darkening with a shadow of regret. "They either widen… or they get sealed."

The café grew quieter, the ambient hum fading as if the world itself held its breath. Aisha's gaze dropped to the note book, its pages filled with scribbled truths she'd only half-understood until now. She reached for it, hesitating as her fingers brushed the worn leather cover. "You've known this all along, haven't you? That they'd come for us."

"I've suspected," Elias said, sliding the notebook toward her. "I've seen their edges—felt their pull. They don't like variables, Aisha. People who see beyond the script. I've been waiting for them, planting the seeds. This—" He tapped the notebook again— "is for those who come after. A map through the shadows."

She flipped it open, her eyes scanning the cryptic notes— diagrams of interlocking circles, phrases that danced between poetry and warning: *The world bends to belief. Reaction is surrender. Choice is freedom.* Her fingers lingered on a sketch of a key, its edges worn as if drawn and redrawn countless times, a symbol of something she couldn't yet grasp.

"What's this for?" she asked, tracing the lines with a trembling finger.

Elias leaned back, his gaze drifting to the window where the city's lights pulsed like a heartbeat. "A door," he said. "One they can't lock. Not yet."

Aisha's breath caught. She wanted to ask more—what door, where it led, why it mattered—but the air shifted again, sharper this time, a vibration rattling the cups on the table. Her head snapped up, eyes wide with panic. "They're here."

Elias stood, his movements swift despite his age, a flicker of urgency breaking his calm. "Go," he said, his voice firm. "Now. Don't look back."

She grabbed the notebook, clutching it to her chest as she bolted for the door. Her coat flared behind her, her boots pounding the worn floorboards. She paused at the threshold, glancing back at Elias, who stood unmoving, his silhouette framed against the dim light. "What about you?"

"I'll be fine," he said, a wry grin breaking through the tension. "I've danced with shadows before. They're terrible partners."

Aisha managed a faint smile despite the fear clawing at her chest, then pushed through the door into the evening. The city swallowed her, its hum rising around her like a tide. She didn't stop running, the notebook a lifeline in her trembling hands, its weight both a burden and a promise.

Back in the café, Elias remained still, the silence settling like dust after a storm. The hum grew louder, a low roar vibrating through the walls, the lights flickering wildly as shadows stretched unnaturally toward him. He picked up his pen, his hand steady as he wrote one final line: *The boy will come soon. He'll need to leap.*

The door chimed again, but no one entered. The lights steadied, and when they did, Elias was gone, the notebook left behind on the table, waiting for the one it was meant for. Outside, the city pulsed on, oblivious to the dance unfolding in its depths—a dance of belief and defiance, of shadows and seekers, of a future yet unwritten.

Contents

Chapter - 1
The Unlived Life

"The world is not happening to you.
It is responding to you."

— Anonymous

The Era Of Silent Expectations

The year was 2042, a time when the future felt like a promise half-kept. Hovercars didn't hum through the skies as old sci-fi had dreamed, but technology had woven itself into every seam of life—holographic billboards pulsed with ads tailored to your thoughts, neural-linked watches buzzed with updates before you even asked, and drones delivered coffee faster than you could brew it. Yet beneath this shimmering veneer, humanity lingered in a quiet limbo, caught between ambition and a bone-deep apathy that no algorithm could fix. Success was still the golden calf—measured in credits, followers, and the glow of a curated digital life—but for every influencer smiling on a screen, a dozen others stared blankly at theirs, lost in the silent expectations of a world that demanded everything and offered little in return.

Most followed the script: school bled into college, college into a job with a steady pulse of income, then marriage, kids, and a rinse-repeat cycle that stretched into the horizon. Dreams were filed away under "someday," passion swapped for practicality like a trade-in at a dealership. Families still existed, tethered by blood, but closeness had frayed—dinners replaced by pings on a chat app, conversations distilled into emojis and likes. It wasn't despair that defined 2042; it was the absence of something vital, a hollow space where meaning should have been.

For Ray Carter and Leila, this world was a cage with invisible bars. They didn't hate it—not exactly. They just couldn't breathe in it. The predictability gnawed at them, the unspoken rules piling up like bricks until the weight felt unbearable. They weren't rebels in the loud, fist-shaking sense; they were quiet renegades, haunted less by failure than by the fear of never truly starting.

The Rooftop That Started It All

Ray Carter was nineteen, a college dropout with a resume that read like a blank page and a mind that spun like a top on the edge of tipping over. Two years ago, he'd been a high school senior teetering on a literal edge—a rooftop above the city, the wind tugging at his jacket as he stared down at the sprawl of lights below. He hadn't planned to jump, not in any concrete way. It was more a test, a dare to himself to feel something—anything—beyond the dull hum of nothing that echoed in his chest. The world stretched out beneath him, a glitter of possibility he couldn't touch, and he'd wondered if it mattered at all. If he mattered.

That's when Leila found him.

She hadn't come running with sirens or panic, no dramatic rescue in the Hollywood sense. She'd just strolled up, her sneakers scuffing the gravel, and leaned against the railing beside him like they were old friends catching a sunset. "If you jump," she'd said, her voice dry as desert sand, "I'll have to figure out this mess alone. And honestly? That sounds exhausting."

Ray had blinked, his brain tripping over her words. "Figure out... what?"

"Life," she'd replied, like it was the dumbest question she'd ever heard. She pulled a half-melted chocolate bar from her pocket, unwrapped it with a crinkle, and held it out. "Want some?"

He'd stared at her—curly hair spilling from a loose bun, brown eyes sharp with something he couldn't name—and felt the absurdity of it all crash over him. Here he was, contemplating the void, and this stranger was offering him candy like they were at a picnic. He didn't know why, but he stepped back from the ledge, took the chocolate, and bit into it. It tasted like sugar and second chances.

They'd been inseparable since.

Leila never asked why he'd been up there, and Ray never told her. The silence between them held it all—the unspoken pact that she'd pulled him back, and he'd let her. She became his tether, the one who saw through his fog and refused to let him drift away. He didn't get why she bothered. Maybe she saw a spark in him he couldn't, buried under layers of doubt. Or maybe she just hated waste—wasted time, wasted lives—and Ray was her latest project. Either way, she'd made it her mission to drag him into the world, kicking and overthinking all the way.

Ray Carter, The Observer

Ray wasn't sure what nineteen was supposed to feel like, but most days, he carried the weight of a thousand unlived lifetimes. He wasn't shy—people mistook his quiet for that—but he'd mastered blending into the background, a shadow in a crowd of holograms. Tall and lean, with messy black hair that looked like he'd lost a fight with a pillow, he moved through life like someone who'd surrendered before the battle started. His dark eyes were dull, glazed with the exhaustion of too much thinking and too little doing. He wasn't sad, not in the textbook sense. He ate, scrolled feeds, laughed at memes about the end of the world—he just… wasn't.

His apartment was a testament to that inertia: a single room with a bed shoved against a cracked wall, a desk drowning in takeout wrappers and half-read books, a window that stared out at a city he barely recognized as home. Each morning, he woke to the same chipped ceiling, promising himself that *tomorrow* he'd do something—apply for a job, write the novel he'd dreamed up in high school, call his parents who'd stopped asking why he'd quit college. But tomorrow never came. Today was just another loop of nothing—a video binge here, a doom-scroll there, a nap to kill the hours. He wasn't depressed, he told himself. He was just waiting. For what, he didn't know.

Leila was the opposite—a storm wrapped in skin, twenty years old and vibrating with a purpose Ray couldn't fathom. Her curly brown hair was always tied back, a chaotic bun that matched her energy, and her sharp brown eyes cut through every excuse like a laser. She didn't shout her presence, but you couldn't ignore it—she walked into a room and the air shifted, as if the world tilted slightly to accommodate her. Where Ray lived in his head, Leila lived in the now, embracing uncertainty like it was an old friend. He saw a void; she saw a blank slate.

And for reasons Ray couldn't grasp, she'd decided he was worth pulling out of his own abyss.

Their friendship was a tangle of push and pull. Leila dragged him into reality—out of his apartment, away from his spiralling thoughts—and Ray resisted, questioning her every move with a cynicism that grated on her nerves. She'd call him out, he'd deflect with a smirk, and somehow, they'd stay tethered. He needed her belief in him, a lifeline he didn't deserve. She needed his stubborn doubt, a reminder of why she fought so hard to live. Opposites, yes, but they fit—like a key and a lock neither knew they'd been searching for.

A Day Like Any Other—Until It Wasn't

Ray had perfected existing without living. This morning was no different: he woke to the buzz of his neural-linked watch, ignored it, and stared at the ceiling until the cracks blurred into shapes—faces, maps, nothing at all. His phone pinged on the cluttered nightstand, a relic from when he'd still bothered to charge it regularly. He let it buzz twice more before glancing at the screen.

Leila: *Get up, loser. You promised you'd come to the bookstore today. I'm not taking no for an answer.*

A smirk tugged at his lips. Of course, she wasn't. Leila didn't do "no." She was a force of nature—hurricane Leila, category relentless—and he was the crumbling shore she kept battering against.

Ray: *Not today. Existential crisis. Try again tomorrow.* He disconnected the phone.

The reply was instant, as if she'd been waiting to pounce. His phone rang before he could blink, her name flashing like a warning. He considered letting it go to voicemail, but that'd just mean she'd show up at his door with that look—half-exasperation, half-determination—and he'd cave anyway. With a groan, he picked up.

"You're not having an existential crisis, Ray," Leila said, cutting him off before he could muster a hello. "You *are* an existential crisis."

He smiled despite himself, running a hand through his tangle of hair. "Good morning to you too, Leila."

"Get up. Meet me at the bookstore in twenty minutes."

"I was planning on staring at my ceiling all day, actually."

"Change of plans. Stare at books instead."

He hesitated, the familiar weight of inertia pressing down. "I don't really feel like—"

"You never feel like it," she interrupted, her voice sharp but not unkind. "That's exactly why you should."

Ray sighed, glancing at the ceiling as if it might offer an escape. "Why do you even bother?"

A beat of silence, then her tone softened—just enough to catch him off guard, she knew which button to press when. "Because someone has to. And I'm not watching you waste away when I know you're better than this."

She hung up before he could argue, leaving the line dead and his excuses dangling. He stared at the phone, then swung his legs over the bed's edge, the cracked floor cold against his feet. Fine. One outing wouldn't kill him. Probably.

The Weight of Nothing

Ray shuffled through his morning routine on autopilot—splashing water on his face, tugging on a hoodie that smelled vaguely of yesterday's takeout, grabbing his keys from a pile of junk mail he hadn't opened. The city outside his window buzzed with life—drones whirring overhead, holo-ads flashing personalized deals (today was a discount on a neural implant he'd never afford)—but it all felt like static, a hum he'd tuned out long ago. He locked the door behind him, the click echoing in the empty hall, and stepped into the street.

The walk to the bookstore was a blur of familiarity: the boutique with its flickering sign, the corner where a glitchy AI street performer played synthetic beats for spare credits, the alley where he'd once scrawled. His thoughts looped as he walked—same as always, a nonstop loop of what-ifs and why-nots. What if he'd stayed in college? What if he'd chased that novel idea instead of letting it rot in a notebook? What if he'd jumped that night, and Leila hadn't been there? The questions never answered anything; they just spun faster, piling up like debt he couldn't pay off.

He didn't notice how much he'd slowed until a drone buzzed too close, its delivery hatch snapping him back to the present. He muttered a curse, sidestepping as it zipped off, and checked his watch. Twenty-six minutes. Leila would give him hell for that.

The Coffee That Changed Everything

The bookstore's wooden doors creaked as Ray pushed them open, the scent of old paper and roasted beans hitting him like a memory he couldn't place. It was a relic in 2042, a stubborn holdout against the digital tide—shelves groaning with physical books, a rarity when most read via neural feeds. The place was quiet, except for the soft hum of classical music and the occasional flip of a page. Leila sat in their usual corner, sprawled in an oversized armchair, smirking over a book like she'd just won an argument with it.

"Twenty-six minutes," she said without looking up. "You're late."

Ray rolled his eyes, collapsing into the chair opposite her. "I was debating whether to show up."

"And yet, here you are."

He sighed, staring at the ceiling—wood-panelled here, not cracked, but just as unhelpful. "Yeah. Here I am."

Leila grinned, setting her book down. "Progress."

The café nook smelled like stories and caffeine, a sanctuary Leila had claimed long before Ray stumbled into her orbit. A battered copy of the book named *The Simulation Hypothesis* sat between them, its cover creased from her grip. She raised an eyebrow, flipping it open. "You actually believe this stuff?"

Ray shrugged, slouching deeper into the chair. "Makes more sense than reality, doesn't it? What if life's just code running in some cosmic server? What if none of it matters?"

Leila frowned, her sharp eyes narrowing. "And what if it does? What if your world's a reflection of what you focus on?"

He opened his mouth to argue—same old dance, him doubting, her pushing—but a deep, controlled and commanding voice cut through the air before he could.

"You're both right. And both completely wrong."

Ray turned, his pulse ticking up a notch. An old man sat at the next table, watching them with eyes that seemed to pierce through the dim light. Silver hair framed a weathered face, a neatly trimmed beard adding a scholarly edge, but it was his presence that unnerved Ray—quiet, heavy, like he'd been waiting there all along, unnoticed until now. He didn't fidget or glance away; he just stared, as if he'd already mapped their conversation in his head.

"Excuse me?" Ray said, frowning.

The man smiled, a slow curve that didn't reach his eyes. "Hello, I am Elias. The world isn't real in the way you think it is. It's not something happening to you—it's something you're creating."

Ray's frown deepened. "That's ridiculous. I don't control the world."

"Not directly," the man said, leaning forward, his voice low and deliberate. "But your thoughts do. Everything you focus on, you attract. Your beliefs shape your reality. And the only thing that has power over you is what you choose to react to."

Leila leaned in, scepticism curling her lips. "Sounds like self-help nonsense."

The man chuckled, a dry sound that carried years of knowing with experience. "Truth often does sound like that. But that doesn't make it any less real."

Ray rolled his eyes, slumping back. "So, what—you're saying if I 'think positive,' my life magically fixes itself?"

"No," the man replied, shaking his head. "I'm saying your world is built by what you constantly and genuinely believe in. Expect misery, you'll find it. Expect failure, you'll create it. Believe nothing matters, and nothing will."

Ray scoffed, crossing his arms. "That's not how reality works."

"Isn't it?" The man's gaze sharpened, pinning Ray in place. "Think of a time you expected something to go wrong, it did go wrong. Didn't it?"

Ray hesitated, his mind flicking to a dozen moments— missed buses he'd predicted, arguments he'd braced for, opportunities he'd assumed would flop. "Well… yeah, but—."

"And when you expected something to go right?"

Silence. Ray had no answer, and that unnerved him more than the man's words. He shifted in his seat, the air suddenly too warm, too close.

The man leaned closer, his voice dropping to a near-whisper. "Perception is reality, Ray. Your thoughts are more powerful than you realize. And the moment you understand that…" He tapped the table once, a deliberate thud. "Your whole world will change."

Ray froze. The man knew his name. How? Leila's eyes flicked between them, her smirk gone, replaced by a flicker of unease. Something about this stranger—his calm, his certainty—felt like a thread pulling at Ray's carefully woven apathy. It wasn't just the words; it was the way he said them, like he'd been waiting for this exact moment, like he'd seen Ray before Ray even saw himself.

"Who are you?" Ray asked, his voice quieter than he meant it to be.

The man's smile widened, but he didn't answer. Instead, he stood, his chair scraping softly against the floor, and walked toward the exit. Ray watched him go, a chill prickling his spine. The man paused at the door, glancing back with those piercing eyes, and gave the slightest nod before mysteriously disappearing into the shadows outside, as if he never existed.

Ray turned to Leila, his pulse thudding. "Did you see that?"

"See what?" She frowned, following his gaze to the empty doorway.

He shook his head, the words tangling in his throat. "Never mind."

But it wasn't nothing. Something had shifted—small, seismic, like a crack in a dam he hadn't known was there. He didn't believe in fate, not really. Yet a tiny, terrifying part of him wondered if fate, or something like it, believed in him.

And as the bookstore hummed around them, oblivious to the tremor in Ray's world, he couldn't shake the feeling that this was only the beginning.

His world was not going to be the same again, ever.

Chapter - 2
Echoes of the Future

"You are not defeated until you stop trying."

— **Anonymous**

A Bookstore, A Question, A Beginning

The bookstore was Leila's sanctuary, a fortress of worn spines and whispered possibilities tucked away from the relentless hum of 2042's cityscape. Holographic billboards pulsed outside, their neural-linked ads chirping into the minds of passersby—*Boost your focus! Only 499 credits!* —but here, the air held the quiet weight of paper and ink, a rebellion against the digital tide. The wooden floors creaked underfoot, the shelves sagged with the burden of forgotten stories, and the faint glow of a single overhead lamp bathed the corner table where Leila sat. To her, this wasn't just a place to escape the world—it was a launchpad to something bigger, a portal to a future she refused to let slip through her fingers. She'd been coming here since she was sixteen, after her brother vanished into the city's labyrinth without a trace, leaving her with a void she'd filled with questions and a stubborn will to keep going. That was four years ago, and ever since she'd hauled Ray off that rooftop, she'd made it her mission to drag him here too—to pull him into the light she'd clawed her way toward.

It wasn't easy. Ray Carter was a puzzle she couldn't quite solve, not yet, he was a storm of quiet chaos wrapped in a hoodie and a smirk. He slumped in the armchair across from her now, his messy black hair falling into his eyes, staring at the table top like it might offer him an exit from his own head. The dim light cast long shadows across his face, highlighting the exhaustion etched into his features—not the kind that came from sleepless nights, but from a life unlived. Leila studied him, her sharp brown eyes narrowing as she sipped her coffee, the steam curling up like a question mark between them.

"So," she said, her voice snapping through the stillness like a whip, "why do you look even more existentially lost than usual?"

Ray sighed, rubbing his temple with a hand that trembled just enough to betray him. "I don't know, Leila. Maybe I'm just… tired. Of everything."

"You say that every week," she shot back instantly, setting her cup down with a deliberate clink. "It's getting old."

"Because it's true every week," he muttered ritualistically, his gaze drifting to the window where the city's lights flickered like a taunt.

Leila leaned forward, resting her elbows on the table, her curly bun tilting precariously as she fixed him with a stare that could cut glass. "Okay, let's try something different. If you could do anything—no limits, no expectations, no 'silent rules' bullshit—what would you do?"

Ray blinked, caught off guard by the question's weight. "What?"

"You heard me." Her tone softened, but her eyes didn't waver. "If you weren't stuck in this cycle of nothing, what would you do?"

He opened his mouth, then closed it, the words dissolving before they could form. The question felt too big, too raw, like a spotlight shining into corners he'd kept dark. "I… I don't know."

Leila sighed, a dramatic exhale that bordered on theatrical. "You can't even imagine wanting something? Damn, Ray. That's depressing."

"I never said I didn't want anything," he snapped, a flicker of defensiveness breaking through his haze. "I just don't know how to want something enough to do anything about it."

She tilted her head, studying him like he was a book she couldn't decide whether to shelve or burn. "That's the problem, then. You keep waiting for purpose to knock on your door like some delivery drone. But maybe you've got to go looking for it, find it. And for that, you've got to move."

She took another sip of her coffee, the faintest smirk tugging at her lips as she continued, "I read somewhere that the most dangerous phrase in life is 'I don't know.' Because as long as you stay there, you're not going anywhere. Indecision is worse than wrong decision. There isn't anything as failure, you either win or learn, you never lose Ray."

Ray scoffed, slumping deeper into his chair. "And what, you've got it all figured out?"

Leila's smirk widened, but there was a glint of something deeper in her eyes—something haunted. "Of course not. But at least I'm trying. Direction is more important than the speed. I may not be there yet Ray, but eventually I will be there. After—" She hesitated, her fingers tightening around her cup, then forged ahead. "After my brother disappeared, I could've sat there, waiting for answers to come that never came. But I didn't. I got up. I started asking questions. I made a choice, I decided that I wasn't going to let life just happen to me. I took the responsibility of my life. I chose my path, I not only made the choice, I took the responsibility of my choice as well."

Ray's smirk faded, replaced by a flicker of curiosity. She rarely talked about her brother—only hints dropped like crumbs, enough to know it had broken something in her but hadn't stopped her. "What happened to him?"

Leila's gaze dropped to her coffee, her voice quieter now, threaded with a rawness she usually kept buried. "I don't know. One day he was here—laughing, planning these wild trips we'd take together—and the next, he was gone. No note, no trace, no clue. Just… nothing. I was sixteen, Ray. I waited for him to come back, thinking he'd walk through the door any minute. He never did. So, I stopped waiting. I started living—for both of us."

Ray swallowed, the weight of her words settling over him like dust. He'd always known Leila was driven, but this— this was the fire behind it. She wasn't just pushing him to live for his sake; she was fighting a battle she'd inherited, a promise to a ghost she couldn't let go.

Noticing The Patterns

Ray let out a slow breath, his fingers tracing the chipped rim of his own coffee cup—a cold, untouched relic of his apathy. Leila's words lingered, sharp and insistent, pricking at the edges of his carefully built numbness. As much as he wanted to deflect, to drown her out with cynicism, a small voice in his head whispered that she might be right. Lately, his life had felt like a scratched holo-disc stuck on repeat: wake up, scroll through dystopian feeds predicting humanity's collapse, avoid the world, sleep, repeat. He was living his life in a rut. He expected things to go wrong, and they did—not just once in a while, over and over again as if a script is being repeated with minor variations, a script he couldn't escape. Relationships fizzled before they began. Job applications vanished into the void of automated rejections. Motivation slipped through his fingers like sand, the tighter he tried to hold the sand the faster it ran out of his hand. Was it all just coincidence, or was there something more to it?

A memory flickered to life—his high school physics teacher droning on about the *observer effect in quantum mechanics, how observing a particle changed its state.* Back then, it had sounded like sci-fi nonsense, a fun fact to toss around at parties he never went to. But now, it clawed at him. What if his expectations were doing the same thing—not to particles, but to his life? What if every time he braced for failure, he was collapsing some unseen wave of possibility into a predictable, miserable outcome?

He thought of the date he'd botched last month. He'd matched with a girl named Priya on a neural-linked app— sharp-witted, with a grin that lit up her profile pic. They'd planned to meet at a rooftop bar, one of those trendy spots with drone-delivered cocktails and a view that made you feel briefly infinite. Ray had spent the whole day expecting it to flop—convinced she'd find him dull, that he'd stumble over his words, that she'd ghost him mid-drink. By the time he got there, his nerves were a live wire, his palms slick with sweat. Sure enough, he'd spilled his drink ten minutes in, fumbled through awkward silences, and watched her eyes glaze over before she made a polite excuse to leave. He hadn't even texted her after. Why bother? He'd known it wouldn't work.

Then there was the job at the holo-design studio. A friend had tipped him off—entry-level, decent pay, a chance to mess with code and visuals in a way that might've sparked something in him. He'd stared at the application for hours, imagining the rejection before he'd even hit send. *They'll see right through me,* he'd thought. *No experience, no degree, no point.* He'd submitted it half-heartedly, typos and all, and when the polite "We've decided to move forward with other candidates" email landed a week later, he'd shrugged. Expected. Same old story.

Leila tapped his hand, jolting him back to the present. "You're thinking way too hard right now."

"Maybe I should," he said, his voice low, almost to himself. "What if... what if everything's happening because I expect it to?"

Her eyes widened, a spark of intrigue flashing across her face. "Now *that's* an interesting thought."

Ray leaned forward, the pieces clicking into place like a puzzle he hadn't known he was solving. "I mean, look at it. Every time I assume something's going to suck, it does. The date with Priya—total disaster because I was already sure it'd be one. The job—I didn't even try because I figured I'd fail. What if it's not just bad luck? What if I'm *making* it happen?"

Leila's smirk returned, but it was softer now, edged with something like pride. "You're starting to sound like me. Except, you know, less optimistic."

He snorted, but the idea wouldn't let go. It was crazy—too simple to explain the mess of his life. And yet, it fit very well. Like a glitch in the code of reality, one he'd been feeding with every doubt-soaked thought.

Glimpse Beyond The Present

Ray exhaled, watching Leila flip through the book in her hands—a battered copy of something called *The Unseen Thread*, its cover faded to a dull grey. She was always digging through the stacks, hunting for ideas that reached beyond the mundane, while he sat there drowning in it. She wasn't content to float through life like he was—she was a diver, plunging into the deep end while he lingered on the shore.

"Alright," he said, breaking the silence, "what about you? If you could do anything, what would it be?"

Leila's expression shifted, a rare hesitation flickering across her face. She set the book down, her fingers lingering on its spine. "I want to change the world."

Ray raised an eyebrow, leaning back with a half-smirk. "That's vague."

"Yeah, well, the specifics keep changing," she admitted, her voice softening as she stared at the table. "Sometimes it's starting a movement, getting people to wake up and fight for something real. Sometimes it's finding him—my brother—and figuring out what happened. But I know one thing: I don't want to wake up one day and realize I've wasted my life being afraid to try. I will be happy to live a life in which I gave my best, every single day, irrespective of the outcome. You can't always be the best but, you can always be at your best. If the process is correct, result is just a matter of time. I surely won't live a life having the regret of not trying."

Her words hung between them, heavy with a longing Ray hadn't heard from her before. He looked down at his coffee, the cold surface rippling slightly as his hand brushed the cup. "Must be nice. Knowing."

Leila reached over, tapping the table with a force that made him jump. "You could know too, Ray. If you stopped being so afraid of failing. You're not a lost cause—you're just stuck. And I'm not letting you stay there."

He wanted to argue, to tell her she didn't get it, that his failures weren't just fear but proof he wasn't cut out for more. But the truth was, she *did* get it—better than he ever had. She'd lost someone, same as he'd lost himself, and instead of sinking, she'd built a ladder out of the wreckage. She was like an intact boat, floating despite water being all around. He was like a boat with a hole it in, water seeping into it. What had he done with his own broken pieces? Nothing so far.

A Mysterious Book and An Unexpected Offer

Leila suddenly sat up straighter, her eyes lighting up as she reached into her bag. "Speaking of waking up…" She pulled out a book—older than the rest, its leather cover cracked and peeling, its pages yellowed like they'd been forgotten for decades. "I found this in the back section. No barcode, no publisher. Just… this."

Ray raised an eyebrow, his curiosity piqued despite himself. "And?"

She slid it across the table with a grin that promised trouble. "Read the first page."

Reluctantly, he flipped the cover open, the faint creak of the spine echoing in the quiet. His eyes scanned the words, handwritten in a jagged scrawl that sent a chill down his spine:

To the one who finds this book: The world is not as it seems. If you are reading this, you have been chosen. There is something greater waiting beyond the ordinary. But first, you must be willing to see beyond what you believe to be real.

A small, tarnished key slipped from between the pages, clattering onto the table with a dull thud. Ray frowned, picking it up. "What is this? Some kind of prank?"

Leila shrugged, her grin widening. "That's what I thought at first too. But keep reading."

He turned the page, his breath catching as more cryptic lines unfolded—symbols he didn't recognize, sketches of interlocking circles, and then a passage that hit him like a punch to the gut:

We do not live in a world of solid reality, but a world of thoughts shaping reality. What you constantly think of, you become. The universe does not respond to who you pretend to be; it responds to the energy you create within. It doesn't matter whether you think you can or cannot, you are right, either way.

Ray's fingers tightened on the book. He and Leila had tossed around ideas like this before—late-night rants over coffee about whether thoughts could bend the world, half-joking debates that always ended with him calling it nonsense. But here it was, inked onto these pages like a confirmation of their wildest theories. His pulse quickened as he flipped further, landing on a shaky scrawl at the bottom of a page:

Meet me at midnight. The rooftop. Come alone.

He looked up at Leila, his voice tight. "Tell me you didn't write this."

She held up her hands, her grin morphing into something more serious. "Swear on my coffee addiction, I didn't. But don't you think it's… strange? Like, what if someone really left this for a reason?"

Ray shook his head, his cynicism warring with a growing unease. "You watch too many conspiracy vids."

"Maybe," she said, leaning closer, her voice dropping to a conspiratorial whisper. "But you've got to admit, this is intriguing. And you need some intrigue in your life, Ray."

He hesitated, his fingers tracing the jagged ink. *Meet me at midnight.* The words pulsed with a quiet urgency, tugging at something deep inside him—a flicker of curiosity he hadn't felt in years. As they debated, a faint shuffle behind them made Ray glance over his shoulder. His breath caught. Elias,the old man from yesterday—the silver-haired stranger with the piercing eyes who'd spouted riddles about perception—stood near the exit, barely visible in the dim light. He hadn't noticed him come in, hadn't seen him sitting there. But those eyes locked onto Ray's, sharp, piercing and unyielding, and for a heartbeat, it felt like everyone and everything disappeared, the room shrank to just the two of them.

The man gave the slightest nod, a gesture loaded with meaning Ray couldn't decipher, then slipped through the door and melted into the night. Ray turned back to Leila, his voice unsteady. "Did you see that?"

She frowned, craning her neck toward the empty doorway. "See what?"

He shook his head, the chill settling deeper. "Never mind."

But it wasn't nothing. The man—Elias, he'd called himself—had been watching, waiting. And now this book, this key, this message… it was too much to dismiss as coincidence. Ray's grip tightened on the leather cover, the weight of it grounding him even as his mind spun.

"So," Leila said, her voice pulling him back, light but edged with intent, "are you coming with me, or not?"

Ray exhaled, glancing at the window where the city stretched out—predictable, routine, suffocating. But something about this moment felt different, like a crack in the script he'd been living. They left the bookstore together, stepping into the cool night air, but not before Ray stole one last look at the spot where Elias had stood.

The chill lingered, a whisper of something bigger brushing against his senses.

Leila nudged him as they walked, her grin infectious. "Still doubting this is something special?"

"I don't know," he said, the words tasting less hollow than usual.

"That's the last time you're saying that," she teased. "Midnight, Ray. This is just the beginning."

"Midnight," he murmured, the key heavy in his pocket. "Alright. Let's see where this goes."

Her grin widened. "That's the spirit."

The Pieces Moving

As they disappeared into the night, a figure watched from the shadows across the street—silver hair glinting faintly under a streetlamp, a knowing smile curling his lips. Elias folded his hands behind his back, his gaze tracking Ray's retreating form. The boy was waking up, slowly but surely, tugging at threads the framework couldn't afford to let unravel. The note Ray had found—that warning— was only the first move. They'd try harder next time.

But Elias had seen something in Ray, something rare: a spark that could ignite a fire they couldn't extinguish. The pieces were moving now, the dance beginning. He turned, melting into the shadows, his footsteps silent against the pavement.

That night, Ray lay in bed, the book on his nightstand a quiet challenge he couldn't ignore. The key rested beside it, its tarnished surface catching the moonlight. He flipped the cover open again, rereading the scrawled words: *Meet me at midnight.* His heart thudded, a mix of dread and anticipation coiling in his chest.

What if this was real? What if this was the turning point he'd never seen coming? The failures—the date, the job, the endless loop of nothing—flashed through his mind, each one a brick in a wall he'd built himself. But what if he could tear it down? What if this book, this key, this midnight meeting was the first crack?

Ray closed his eyes, the city's hum a distant lullaby. Midnight. He had a choice to make—one he couldn't unmake. And for the first time in years, he wasn't sure he wanted to stay where he was.

The clock ticked closer, the shadows deepening. Whatever waited on that rooftop, he'd face it. Not as the observer he'd been, but as something new.

Something more.

Chapter - 3
The Midnight Meeting

"We cannot always control the situation and actions of others, but we can always control our reactions to them."

— Anonymous

A Night of Restlessness

Ray Carter lay sprawled across his narrow bed, the cracked ceiling of his apartment staring back at him like a map of his fractured thoughts. The faint hum of 2042 pulsed beyond his window—a city alive with neural-linked drones, holographic billboards whispering personalized ads into the minds of passersby, and the relentless buzz of a world that never slept. Inside, though, the silence was deafening, broken only by the occasional creak of the building settling or the distant wail of a siren slicing through the night. The clock on his nightstand glowed 11:32 PM, its red digits ticking closer to midnight with a quiet inevitability that made his chest tighten.

Sleep eluded him, as it often did these days. His mind churned, a restless tide pulling him under waves of doubt, curiosity, and something he couldn't name—something that had taken root since that encounter in the bookstore. The key he'd found in the mysterious book rested beside the clock, its tarnished surface catching the faint streetlight filtering through his blinds. It was small, unremarkable, yet it felt like a weight pressing against his ribs, a tangible tether to the questions he couldn't shake. *Meet me at midnight. The rooftop. Come alone.* The words scrawled in jagged ink replayed in his head, each syllable a drumbeat urging him toward a choice he wasn't sure he was ready to make.

He rolled onto his side, the mattress groaning under his weight, and stared at the key. You are the average of five people you interact with most. In Ray's case, it was just Leila. Leila's excitement had been infectious earlier, her grin lighting up the café as she'd pushed him to see this as an adventure, a break from the monotony that had defined his life for too long. "This is your chance, Ray," she'd said, her voice sharp with conviction. "Something big. Don't let it slip away, grab it with both hands Ray." But now, alone in the dim glow of his room, the bravado he'd borrowed from her faded. What if this was nothing? A prank, a delusion, a waste of time? What if he was chasing shadows only to find more emptiness on the other side?

Ray sat up, swinging his legs over the bed's edge, the cold floor jolting him further awake. His fingers brushed the key, its edges rough against his skin. He clenched it in his fist, the metal biting into his palm as he paced the cramped space. The room felt smaller tonight, its walls closing in like a trap he'd built himself. Posters peeled from the corners—a faded band he'd once loved, a sci-fi movie he'd watched a dozen times—mocking reminders of a life he'd let stagnate. His desk was a graveyard of half-finished ideas: a notebook with a novel's opening line scratched out, a stack of job applications he'd never sent, a neural-linked watch he hadn't bothered to charge in weeks. This was his world—predictable, safe, suffocating—and he hated it.

Yet the alternative terrified him more. That old man— Elias—had spoken with a certainty that gnawed at Ray's scepticism. "Your thoughts shape your reality," he'd said, as if it were a law as immutable as gravity and death. Ray had laughed it off then, but the failures he'd catalogued earlier today—the botched date, the rejected job—kept circling back, each one a brick in a wall he'd constructed with his own doubts. What if Elias was right? What if this midnight meeting wasn't just a whim but a crack in that wall, a chance to see beyond the script he'd been living?

He stopped pacing, his reflection flickering in the smudged glass of his window. The city outside was a kaleidoscope of light and shadow, drones weaving through the air like fireflies, their neural feeds syncing with the minds below. It was beautiful in its chaos, a future he'd once dreamed of being part of—back when dreams still felt possible. Now, it just felt like noise, a relentless reminder of everything he wasn't. But tonight, something stirred in him, a flicker of the boy who'd stood on a rooftop two years ago, daring himself to feel alive. Leila had pulled him back from going into the abyss, then. Now, maybe this was her pushing him forward towards the rainbow.

Ray exhaled, shoving the key into his pocket. Whether this was real or a fool's errand, he had to know. He grabbed his jacket, the fabric worn thin at the elbows, and slipped out into the night, the door clicking shut behind him with a finality that echoed in his bones.

The Rooftop

The stairwell smelled of damp concrete and rust, each step reverberating with the hollow thud of his boots as he climbed toward the rooftop Leila had suggested—an abandoned building a few blocks from his apartment, its silhouette a jagged scar against the bruised sky. The air grew crisper as he ascended, the city's hum fading into a distant murmur, replaced by the whistle of wind through broken windows. His breath misted in front of him, his pulse quickening with each floor. He didn't know what he'd find up there—Elias, answers, nothing at all—but the uncertainty fuelled him now, a strange mix of dread and exhilaration coiling in his gut.

The rooftop door creaked as he pushed it open, a gust of frigid air slapping his face. The city sprawled before him, a sea of glowing windows and flickering holo-ads painting the night in neon streaks. Drones zipped overhead, their AI lenses glinting like predatory eyes, while below, the streets pulsed with life—self-driving cabs weaving through traffic, pedestrians synced to their neural feeds, oblivious to the world beyond their screens. It was 2042 in all its chaotic glory, a future Ray had once marvelled at from afar, now a backdrop to the unease tightening his chest.

Leila was already there, perched on the ledge like a bird ready to take flight, her legs dangling over the edge. Her curly hair whipped in the wind, her silhouette framed against the skyline as she tossed a pebble into the abyss below. She didn't turn as he approached, but her voice cut through the stillness, sharp and teasing. "Took you long enough."

Ray stepped closer, gravel crunching under his boots. "I almost didn't come."

She smirked, finally glancing at him, her sharp brown eyes glinting with mischief. "But you did. That's what matters. Better late than never."

He stopped beside her, shoving his hands into his pockets to hide their trembling. The key felt heavier now, a silent question pressing against his thigh. They sat in silence for a moment, the city's hum filling the space between them, a rhythm as familiar as their friendship. Leila's presence steadied him, her unshakable resolve a lifeline he clung to when his own faltered. But tonight, even she couldn't quiet the storm in his head.

Footsteps echoed from the stairwell, deliberate and measured. Ray tensed, his breath catching as a figure emerged from the shadows—Elias. The old man's silver hair gleamed under the faint rooftop light, his coat billowing slightly in the wind. He carried himself with the same quiet command Ray remembered from the bookstore, his presence a weight that seemed to bend the air around him.

"You're right on time," Elias said, his voice was gravelly, deep and commanding, but calm, as if he'd all along known that eventually Ray would show. He looked assured.

Ray clenched the key in his fist, its edges biting into his palm. "For what?"

Elias took a deep breath, his sharp grey eyes locking onto Ray's with an intensity that made him feel transparent. "For the truth."

The Truth About Reality

Elias gestured for them to follow, leading them toward the centre of the rooftop where the wind swirled colder, tugging at their clothes. Ray hesitated, glancing at Leila, who gave him a subtle nod—her way of saying she was in this with him, no matter what. They moved closer, gravel shifting underfoot, the city's glow casting long shadows that danced around them like spectres.

"You've started to see the patterns, haven't you, Ray?" Elias asked, his tone steady but probing.

Ray nodded slowly, the failures he'd dissected earlier flashing through his mind—Priya's fading smile, the job rejection email, the countless times he'd expected the worst and watched it unfold. "Yeah. It's like… everything bad happens because I expect it to. But that can't be real, right? Life isn't that simple."

Elias gave a small, all knowing smile, the lines on his weathered face deepening. "Ah, but it is. The world isn't made of solid facts—it's made of perceptions. Your thoughts shape your reality more than you realize. Most people drift through life reacting to circumstances, never grasping that their reactions are the only true power they have."

Leila crossed her arms, her scepticism cutting through the wind's howl. "So, what you're saying is, we can just think our problems away? That's a little too 'self-help guru' for me."

Elias chuckled, a dry sound that carried years of experience. "No, Leila. I'm saying that when you change how you see the world, the world itself changes. Your perception is a lens—everything you experience filters through it. If you expect failure, you'll find failure. If you expect opportunity, you'll recognize it when it comes. It's not magic—it's focus. What you pay attention to, what you focus on will get powerful. We all have two wolves always fighting within us, the good one and the bad one."

Leila asked curiously, "Which one wins?"

Elias said, "The one you feed. Our mind obeys our desires. If you expect problems, the mind will show them everywhere. However, if you look for solutions, you find them too. What you focus on is your choice, after all, it's your life."

Ray frowned, his mind wrestling with the idea. "So, you're saying life's like a mirror? It reflects back what we put into it?"

"Exactly," Elias said, his voice firm. "Ever notice how two people can face the same event and come away with completely different stories? Take a rejection—say, a job you wanted. One person sees it as proof they're not good enough, lets it spiral into despair. Another sees it as a detour, a chance to pivot to something better, he sees rejection as redirection. The rejection's the same, but the lens changes everything."

Ray's thoughts drifted to his physics teacher's lecture on the observer effect—how observing a quantum particle collapsed its possibilities into a single state. Was that what Elias meant? Was his life a wave of potential, shaped by where he chose to look? "That makes sense," he said slowly. "But what about stuff we can't control? Like if someone screws you over?"

Elias's smile widened, a glint of challenge in his eyes. "You can't control how others act. But you can control whether you let it define you. Picture this: you're walking down the street, and some jerk in a hovercab cuts you off, yelling out the window. You've got two paths—react with anger, let it fester all day, ruin your mood. Or, let it slide, shake it off, keep moving. The cab's the same either way, but your reaction decides what it becomes for you. Pain might hit you, sure—life's messy like that—but suffering? That's optional."

Leila tapped her fingers against her arm, her brow furrowing. "So, you're saying everything's about how we react?"

"Precisely," Elias replied, stepping closer, his voice dropping to a conspiratorial whisper. "People and problems only have power if you give it to them. Look through history—think of someone like... say, that scientist who got locked up for saying the Earth wasn't the centre of everything. Galileo, right? He faced exile, rejection, the whole mess. Most would've broken. But he saw it differently—each blow was just fuel for his truth. His perception didn't just keep him going; it changed the world. He didn't react to the chaos—he shaped it."

Ray exhaled, the weight of Elias's words settling over him like a cloak. His whole life, he'd thought he was a pawn in an indifferent game—bad luck, bad timing, bad everything. But what if he'd been the player all along, moving pieces without realizing it? "So, if I believe my life's pointless... it becomes pointless?"

Elias met his gaze, unflinching. "Yes. And if you believe it has meaning, it will. The choice is yours—it always has been. Irrespective of what you choose, you have to pay the price Ray. You cannot escape from paying the price Ray."

Ray sat back on his heels, the rooftop gravel digging into his knees as he absorbed it all. Leila smirked beside him, her voice breaking the tension. "That's a lot to take in."

Elias's smile returned, warm but edged with something deeper. "It always is. But once you start noticing, you can't stop."

Ray rubbed his temples, his mind spinning with possibilities. "Okay… but that still doesn't explain the book, or the key. Why us?"

Elias reached into his coat, pulling out a folded piece of paper, its edges frayed and ink-smudged. He handed it to Ray, who unfolded it with trembling fingers. The message was stark, scrawled in the same jagged handwriting as the book: *The world you know is only one version of reality. If you're willing to step beyond what you believe, you'll find the truth. But beware—once seen, it cannot be unseen.*

Ray's pulse quickened, a chill racing down his spine. "What does this mean?"

Elias's expression turned unreadable, a shadow passing over his face. "It means your journey's just beginning."

A Door to The Unknown

Elias turned abruptly, striding toward an old, rusted door at the far end of the rooftop—a relic that looked like it hadn't been touched in decades, its paint peeling like shedding skin. Ray and Leila exchanged a glance, her eyes wide with a mix of fear and exhilaration. Elias placed his hand against the metal, and a faint glow pulsed beneath his palm, the air humming with a low, electric charge.

"The key, Ray," Elias said, his voice steady but urgent.

Ray's heart thudded against his ribs. Every instinct screamed at him to turn back—to cling to the safety of his predictable, empty life, where questions stayed unanswered and risks untested. But his heart—his heart told him something else. This was the crack in the wall, the chance to see beyond. With a shaky breath, he stepped forward, pulling the key from his pocket. It felt alive now, buzzing faintly in his grip as he slid it into the lock.

The door clicked open with a sound that echoed like a gunshot in the night.

A rush of air spilled out—warm, charged, smelling faintly of ozone and something ancient. Beyond the threshold wasn't the stairwell Ray expected, nor another rooftop, but... something else. A shimmering void, a distortion of light and shadow that pulsed with an energy he couldn't name. It wasn't a place—it was a possibility.

Leila's breath hitched beside him, her voice barely a whisper. "Ray... what is that?"

He shook his head, his throat dry. "I have no idea."

Elias stepped aside, his smile faint but resolute. "Are you ready to find out?"

Ray looked at Leila, her eyes mirroring his own mix of terror and wonder. She nodded, a silent pact sealing their fates. Without another word, they stepped forward together, crossing the threshold into the unknown. The world tilted, the rooftop fading behind them as light swallowed them whole, and for one fleeting moment, Ray felt weightless—untethered from the life he'd known, suspended in a truth he was only beginning to grasp.

Whatever lay ahead, he'd face it. Not as the observer he'd been, but as something new.

Something more, someone decisive.

Chapter - 4
The First Shift

"When we do something, we become something. We shouldn't do something to get something but to become something. The magic is in the process."

— Anonymous

Crossing The Threshold

Ray's pulse thundered in his ears as he stepped through the rusted rooftop door, Leila's hand brushing his arm as she followed. The air thickened instantly, a warm, electric rush that prickled his skin and made his hair stand on end. It wasn't just a gentle flow of air—it was as if the universe itself had exhaled, acknowledging their crossing with a hum that vibrated through his bones. He barely had time to process the sensation before a blinding light swallowed them whole, searing his vision white. His stomach lurched, a freefall without motion, and then—silence.

When the world steadied, the rooftop was gone. Ray blinked hard, his eyes adjusting to a golden haze that bathed a crowded street. The air smelled different— cleaner, sharper, laced with the faint tang of blooming trees instead of the city's usual exhaust. Voices swirled around him, a chorus of chatter and laughter, but something felt off, like a song played in the wrong key. He turned to Leila, and his breath caught.

She wasn't the Leila he knew—not exactly. Her curly brown hair was cropped shorter, framing her face in unfamiliar waves, and she wore a leather jacket that looked too new, too bold for the Leila who favoured worn hoodies. But it was her eyes that stopped him cold. They held a flicker of confusion, a distance he hadn't seen before, as if she were seeing him for the first time.

"Ray..." Her voice was tentative, testing the word like it might not fit. "What's... what's going on?"

He swallowed hard, his throat dry. "I don't know. Where are we?"

Leila frowned, tilting her head as if the question didn't make sense. "What do you mean? We're right where we're supposed to be."

The words hit him like a punch. Something was terribly wrong.

A Reality Unfamiliar Yet Known

Ray spun in a slow circle, his mind racing to anchor itself. The street stretched before him, lined with buildings he recognized from his hometown—yet they were different. The corner store where he'd bought cheap coffee was now a sleek café with a neon sign that read "Quantum Brew." The old library, usually crumbling and forgotten, stood polished and modern, its glass doors reflecting a bustling crowd. Above them, a towering billboard flashed an advertisement for a tech gadget he'd never heard of: *ThoughtSync X—Live Your Focus*. And beneath it, in bold letters: *June 5, 2038*.

His knees buckled. 2038. Four years in the past.

"Rayan?" Leila's voice cut through his shock, sharper now. "You're freaking me out. What's wrong?"

He turned to her, his voice trembling. "Rayan? I am Ray. Leila, it's 2038. We were in 2042. Don't you see it?"

Her brow furrowed, and she glanced at the billboard as if it were nothing unusual. "Yeah, and I am Sara not Leila, it's June 5th. So, what? We've got plans today—don't tell me you forgot."

"Forgot?" Ray's head spun. "Leila, we just walked through a door on a rooftop. Elias gave me a key, and now we're here. This isn't right."

She stepped back, crossing her arms. "Why you keep calling me Leila? I am Sara. Who's Elias? And what door? Rayan, we've been planning this all week. You've got that interview at Ever Tech today. You've been a mess about it."

"Why are you calling me Rayan Leila? Ever Tech?" The name jolted him. He knew it—a tech giant he'd dreamed of working for but had never dared approach. "I never applied to Ever Tech."

Leila—or whoever she was here—laughed, a sound that was both familiar and alien. "Are you kidding? You've been obsessed with that application for weeks. You stayed up all night tweaking it. I had to drag you out of your apartment to eat something."

Ray's hands shook as he reached into his pockets. His phone was there, but when he unlocked it, the screen glowed with a photo he didn't remember taking—him and Leila, grinning at a concert, lights blazing behind them. His messages were a flood of conversations he'd never had: plans with friends he didn't recognize, a group chat buzzing about a party he hadn't attended. His life here wasn't his—it was someone else's.

A Life That Could Have Been

"Ray, you Okay?" Leila stepped closer, her concern deepening. "You're acting like you've never seen me before."

He forced a nod, his mind reeling. "Yeah, just… nervous."

She grinned, the tension easing from her face. "Well, duh. It's a big deal. But you've got this. Come on, we need to get you to that interview."

Before he could protest, she grabbed his wrist and pulled him down the sidewalk, weaving through a crowd that seemed oblivious to his unravelling reality. As they walked, fragments of this life pieced themselves together in his mind. Ever Tech—an internship he'd landed here, a chance he'd never taken in 2042. A version of himself had made bolder choices, hadn't let fear dictate his steps. But who was he now? Was he still Ray Carter, or someone else entirely?

They stopped at a coffee shop, the same one they'd frequented in 2042, though its sign now read *Brew Beyond*. Leila pushed him toward the counter. "Get your usual. It'll calm you down."

Ray hesitated, unsure what "usual" meant here, but the barista—a young woman with a bright smile—greeted him like an old friend. "Hey, Ryan! Black coffee, no sugar, right?"

Ryan. The name hit him like a brick. He nodded numbly, watching as she scribbled it on a cup. When she handed it over, the ink confirmed it: *Ryan.* Not Ray. His legs felt weak, but he forced himself to take the drink, turning back to Leila.

She was watching him, her expression shifting from worry to suspicion. "Ray—Ryan—what's going on with you?"

"I…" He stumbled over the words, clutching the cup. "I don't think I'm supposed to be here."

"What are you talking about?" She reached for him, but he stepped back, shaking his head.

"I need to figure this out." He bolted out the door, ignoring her call after him. The street blurred as he ran, his mind a storm of questions. Buildings loomed, familiar yet wrong—names changed, facades altered. He spotted a childhood friend across the road—Tommy, who'd moved away years ago—but when Ray shouted his name, Tommy didn't turn. No one did. They didn't know him. Not the real him.

And Leila wasn't his Leila. She was someone else's anchor, tethered to a Ryan who'd lived a life Ray had only dreamed of.

Timeline Depth: The Weight Of What Might Have Been

Ray ducked into an alley, his chest heaving as he pressed his back against the cool brick. This wasn't just a shift in time—it was a shift in who he was. He closed his eyes, and flashes of alternate lives flickered behind his lids, unbidden but vivid.

In one, he saw himself alone, older, hunched over a desk in a dim apartment. The year was 2045, and he'd never left his rut—scrolling feeds of a decaying world, his dreams buried under apathy. Misery clung to him like damp rot, every day a repetition of the last. He'd expected nothing, and nothing was what he'd gotten. The loneliness stung, a hollow ache that made his breath hitch even now.

In another, he was a scientist, standing in a gleaming lab, screens glowing with data he'd spent years decoding. It was 2040, and he'd sacrificed everything—friends, love, rest—to chase a breakthrough: a device that mapped thought patterns, proving reality bent to belief. He'd succeeded, but at a cost. His hands trembled in that vision, his eyes sunken, and when he looked in a mirror, he didn't recognize the man staring back. The weight of that sacrifice pressed against Ray's chest, a lesson in the price of ambition unchecked by balance.

He opened his eyes, gasping. These weren't random glimpses—they were warnings, echoes of paths he could have taken, shaped by what he'd focused on. Elias's words rang in his skull: *Your world is the result of what you focus on.* Was this proof? Had his timid choices in 2042 built one reality, while another Ray—Ryan—had dared more here?

Leila's Adaptation

Footsteps echoed behind him. Leila emerged from the crowd, her leather jacket catching the sunlight. "Ray— Ryan—whatever you're calling yourself today, stop running!"

He froze, guilt twisting his gut. "I'm sorry. I just—"

"No," she interrupted, stepping closer. "You don't get to freak out and leave me guessing. Talk to me."

Her resolve steadied him, even here, in this fractured reality. He exhaled shakily. "This isn't my life, Leila.... Sara. I don't belong here."

She crossed her arms, studying him. "You keep saying that, but you're here. With me. Doesn't that mean something?"

"It does," he admitted. "But you don't remember Elias, the rooftop, the key. I don't know who I am to you."

Her eyes softened, and she reached out, resting a hand on his arm. "You're my best friend, you idiot. You've been there through everything—my breakup, my stupid art projects, all of it. If you're lost, we figure it out together. That's what we do."

The words pierced him, a lifeline across realities. This Leila—Sara, he reminded himself—didn't know the rooftop, but she knew him, or some version of him. Her strength mirrored the Leila he'd left behind, adapting to his chaos with the same fierce loyalty. "Okay," he said, voice steadier. "Together."

She nodded, a flicker of her old grin breaking through. "Good. Now let's get you to that interview before you implode."

The Weight of A Choice

They walked in silence, Ray's mind churning. If this was 2038, and he was Ryan, what did it mean? Had he leapt into a parallel life, or was this a test? Elias's voice echoed again: *Perception is reality*. Maybe this was his chance to see what he could have been—to feel the weight of choices he'd never made.

At EverTech's glass-fronted building, Sara gave him a nudge. "You've got this, Ryan. I'll wait here."

He nodded, stepping inside. The lobby buzzed with energy—holographic displays, voices discussing neural tech. A woman greeted him, clipboard in hand. "Ryan Carter? They're ready for you."

The interview blurred past—questions about coding, his passion for innovation. He answered on instinct, drawing from a confidence he didn't know he had. When it ended, the interviewer smiled. "We'll be in touch. You've got potential."

Potential. The word lingered as he rejoined Sara. She beamed. "Told you you'd nail it."

But doubt gnawed at him. This life—Ryan's life—wasn't his. Or was it? Could he claim it, rewrite his reality here? The thought thrilled and terrified him.

Elias's Warning

Back on the street, a shadow caught his eye. Across the road, Elias stood, his silver hair unmistakable. Ray's heart leapt. "Sara, stay here."

He darted through traffic, reaching Elias as the old man turned to face him. "You made it," Elias said, his voice calm but edged with urgency.

"What is this?" Ray demanded. "Why am I here?"

Elias's eyes darkened. "A lesson. You've seen what your focus can build—or destroy. But this isn't the end."

"What do you mean?"

"There are others," Elias said, glancing skyward as if expecting something. "They watch. They enforce. If you keep pushing, they'll come for you."

"Who?" Ray pressed, but Elias stepped back, fading into the crowd.

"Choose wisely, Ray," he called. "The door's still open."

Ray spun, searching for him, but Elias was gone. Sara caught up, breathless. "Who was that?"

He shook his head, a chill settling over him. "Someone who knows more than he's telling."

The billboard flickered above, *ThoughtSync X* glowing ominously. Ray clenched his fists. This shift wasn't random—it was a test, and something bigger loomed on the horizon. He had to find his way back—or decide if he even wanted to.

He had a choice to make and now he knew very well that he have to pay the price as well, no matter what.

Chapter - 5

The Test

A World That Isn't His

Ray stood frozen on the sidewalk, the bustling street of this alternate 2038 blurring around him. The air carried a crispness he didn't recognize, laced with the scent of blooming trees rather than the exhaust he'd grown accustomed to in 2042. Buildings towered with familiar shapes but unfamiliar names—*Quantum Brew* instead of his usual dive, *ThoughtSync X* flashing on a billboard overhead. Every detail screamed of a life he hadn't lived, a reality where he was *Ryan*, not Ray. His chest tightened, a cocktail of dread and disorientation swirling within him. He'd wanted escape, a break from the monotony that chained him, but not this—not a world where he was a stranger to himself.

Sara—no, Leila, or whatever she was here—stood beside him, her leather jacket gleaming under the midday sun. Her brow furrowed as she watched him, her sharp brown eyes narrowing with concern. "Rayan…. Ray, seriously. What's going on with you? You're acting like you've never seen this place before."

He forced a breath, his voice unsteady. "I haven't. Not like this."

Her frown deepened, but before she could press further, Ray shook his head. He couldn't explain—not yet. Elias had thrust him into this shift, this fracture of reality, for a reason. The old man's words echoed in his skull: *Your world is the result of what you focus on.* If that was true, then this wasn't just a fluke. It was a test. A chance to prove he could wield the power Elias had hinted at—the power to shape his reality through belief, through choice.

"I need to try something," he said, more to himself than to her.

Sara crossed her arms, tilting her head. "Try what?"

He didn't answer. Instead, he closed his eyes, shutting out the noise of the crowd, the hum of hover-cars overhead, the weight of a life he didn't claim. If perception shaped reality, he could bend it—start small, test the edges. He pictured the coffee cup he'd clutched earlier, the one labelled *Ryan* in neat black ink. In his reality, it would've been *Ray*. He'd never expected anything else back home. But what if he had?

He opened his eyes and glanced down at the cup still in his hand, discarded on a nearby bench. The name stared back at him: *Ray*. His breath caught, a jolt of adrenaline surging through him. He did it! It had changed. Subtle, insignificant to anyone else, but to him, it was the proof— his focus had rewritten a fragment of this world. So, the bigger things are possible too!

Sara followed his gaze, her confusion deepening. "What's with the cup?"

He shook his head, a faint grin tugging at his lips. "Nothing. Just... checking something."

Multiple Tests: The Crowd And The Chance

The realization ignited something in him—a spark of curiosity, a hunger to push further. If he could alter a name, what else could he change? He scanned the street, searching for a challenge, something to test the limits of this newfound control. His eyes landed on a knot of people ahead, their voices rising in a chaotic tangle. A street vendor's cart had tipped, spilling fruits and trinkets across the pavement, and the crowd was spiralling—shouts of frustration, a child's wail, a man shoving another aside to grab a rolling apple.

Ray's instinct was to shrink back, to let the disorder wash over him as it always had. In 2042, he'd have seen it as proof of a world gone mad, a mess he couldn't fix. But here, in this test, he saw opportunity. Elias had said it: *People and problems only have power if you let them.* What if he didn't?

He stepped forward, Sara trailing behind with a skeptical, "Ray, what are you doing?"

"Calming it," he muttered, focusing on the scene. He didn't react with panic or judgment. Instead, he envisioned order—a ripple of calm spreading outward, voices softening, hands unclenching. His breath steadied as he held the image, projecting it like a signal into the chaos. At first, nothing shifted; the shouting grew louder, a woman's curse cutting through the din. Doubt crept in, but he shoved it aside. *Believe it*, he told himself. *Expect it.*

Then, slowly, the tide turned. The vendor laughed—a sharp, unexpected sound—and tossed an apple to the man who'd shoved past, defusing the tension. A bystander bent to help gather the scattered goods, others following suit. The child's cries quieted as a stranger offered a trinket, and within moments, the crowd dispersed, the air lighter, the street settling into rhythm again.

Ray exhaled, his hands trembling with a mix of exhaustion and triumph. Sara stared at him, wide-eyed. "Did you… do that?"

"I don't know," he lied, though the truth burned bright within him. He'd done it—not with words or force, but with focus. His perception had nudged reality, just enough to prove Elias right.

But he wasn't done. The crowd was a small victory; he needed something personal, tangible. His mind snagged on Sara's earlier words: *the internship at EverTech*. In his world, he'd never dared apply—fear of rejection had kept him stagnant. Here, Ryan had seized the chance. What if Ray could too?

He turned to Sara, his voice steadier now. "That internship—tell me more. How did I get it?"

She laughed, oblivious to the weight of his question. "You applied, genius. Sent in a killer proposal, aced the interview. You wouldn't shut up about it."

Ray's stomach twisted. In 2042, he'd dismissed EverTech as a pipe dream, expecting failure before he even tried. Here, he'd expected success—and it had come. Could he summon that now? He closed his eyes again, picturing a letter in his pocket—an acceptance he hadn't earned in this moment but could claim through belief. His fingers brushed the fabric of his jeans, hesitant, then dipped inside.

Paper crinkled against his skin. He pulled it out, unfolding a crisp envelope stamped with EverTech's logo. *Congratulations, Ryan Carter. We're pleased to offer you*... His pulse raced, a laugh bubbling up unbidden. Sara snatched it from him, scanning the text.

"This is old news," she said, tossing it back. "You got that weeks ago."

To her, it was history. To him, it was a miracle—a bridge between who he'd been and who he could be.

The Bully That Wasn't

Ray's confidence swelled, but the test wasn't over. As they rounded a corner, a figure loomed ahead, leaning against a lamppost with a lazy arrogance Ray knew too well. Zane Walker—his high school tormentor, broad-shouldered and smirking, a cigarette dangling from his lips. In 2042, Zane had been a shadow over Ray's life, every taunt a confirmation of his worthlessness. Here, in 2038, they'd never crossed paths. Yet there he was, eyes locking onto Ray with a flicker of recognition that shouldn't exist.

"Well, well," Zane drawled, pushing off the post. His voice carried the same venom Ray remembered, though softer, less certain. "Carter. Still think you're better than everyone?"

Ray's gut clenched, old fears surging—memories of shoved lockers, jeering crowds, the sting of knuckles against his cheek. His hands twitched, ready to ball into fists. But then Elias's lesson cut through: *You control your reaction. They have no power unless you give it.*

Sara tensed beside him, whispering, "Ray, let's just go."

"No," he said, planting his feet. He met Zane's gaze—not with anger, not with fear, but with something new: indifference. "I don't know you here, Zane. And you don't know me."

Zane's smirk faltered, his bravado cracking. He stepped closer, close enough that Ray smelled the smoke on his breath, the faint sourness of cheap beer. "You always were a coward. Hiding behind your little friend now?"

Ray saw it then—the tremble in Zane's hand, the hollow edge to his words. This wasn't the bully he'd feared; this was a boy lashing out, desperate for control he didn't have. In 2042, Ray had fed that power with his flinches, his retreat. Not anymore.

"You're wrong," Ray said, voice calm but firm. "I'm not hiding. And you? You're just noise."

Zane blinked, thrown off-balance. He shoved Ray's shoulder, testing him, but Ray didn't budge. He didn't flinch, didn't glare—just stood there, unshaken. The push lacked force, a half-hearted jab from someone who didn't know why he was fighting. Zane muttered a curse, spat on the ground, and turned away, his footsteps fading into the crowd.

Sara exhaled, her tension melting into a grin. "That was… weirdly badass."

Ray's heart pounded, but not from fear—from victory. Zane had no power here, not because he'd changed, but because Ray had. He'd stripped the bully of his hold with a single choice: non-reaction.

Facing Elias: The Guiding Light

The tests had built something in Ray—a foundation he couldn't yet name but could feel, solid and growing. He needed Elias now, needed to understand the scope of what he'd tapped into. "We're going back to the rooftop," he said, turning abruptly.

Sara jogged to keep up, her skepticism plain. "Ray, what's this about?"

"To prove a theory," he replied, his mind already racing ahead. If he expected Elias to be there, he would be. Belief was the key.

The stairwell loomed ahead, the same rusted door from their first shift waiting at the top. Ray pushed it open, heart hammering, and there he was—Elias, silver hair glinting under the sun, standing near the edge as if he'd never left.

"You figured it out," Elias said, his voice warm with approval, though his eyes held a deeper scrutiny.

Ray stepped forward, breathless but resolute. "I think so. It's about what I give power to, isn't it? The cup, the crowd, Zane—I changed them by changing me."

Elias nodded, crossing his arms. "More than that. You're starting to see the thread that ties it all together: your mind isn't just a mirror—it's a sculptor. Reality bends to what you hold steady within you, focus upon."

Ray frowned, processing. "But why me? Why this?"

Elias's gaze softened, a rare vulnerability breaking through. "Because you were ready to ask, Ray. Most drift through life, reacting to shadows they think are solid. You dared to question them. That's where it begins."

"And where does it end?" Ray pressed, the weight of his journey pressing against him.

"It doesn't," Elias said, stepping closer. "This isn't about an end—it's about a beginning. Every choice you make ripples outward. You've stopped letting the world define you. Now, you define it. But it's not easy. Expectation is a muscle—flex it, and it grows. Neglect it, and it withers. *Use it or lose it.*"

Ray glanced at Sara, who watched with a mix of awe and confusion, then back to Elias. "So, what's next?"

Elias smiled, a glint of challenge in his eyes. "You tell me. You've passed the test of reaction. The next one's about creation—what you build with this power. Choose wisely, Ray. The world's watching."

The rooftop stretched silent around them, the city humming below. Ray's fists clenched, not from fear but from resolve. He'd reshaped fragments of this reality— coffee cups, crowds, old ghosts. The test wasn't over; it was evolving. And for the first time, he wasn't just surviving it, he was thriving—he was ready to shape it.

Chapter - 6

The Power of Non-Reaction

"You cannot control the actions of others, but you can control how you react to them. And that is where your true power lies."— **Anonymous**

A Fragile Trust

Ray stood on the rooftop, the city's artificial glow painting the night in hues of amber and steel. The air was cool, carrying the faint hum of 2042—a symphony of drones, distant traffic, and the ever-present buzz of thought-responsive billboards flickering with ads tailored to passersby. Elias's presence beside him was a quiet anchor, his silver hair catching the light as he watched Ray with that knowing gaze. The shift from the last test still lingered in Ray's bones, the weight of his victories over Zane and the altered coffee cup grounding him in a truth he was only beginning to grasp: his reactions shaped his reality as much as his beliefs did.

But that truth felt fragile, untested against the deeper currents of his life. He glanced at the stairwell, half-expecting Leila to burst through, her storm of purpose dragging him into another moment of clarity. She'd been his constant since that night on the rooftop two years ago, the one who'd pulled him back from the edge—literally as well as figuratively. Their friendship wasn't flawless; it was a push-and-pull of her relentless drive and his stubborn inertia. Yet beneath the bickering, there was trust. A trust forged in late-night talks at the café, in the shared dream of a mural project they'd started last summer—a chaotic swirl of colours meant to brighten their grey hometown. She'd sketched the outlines, he'd mixed the paints, and together they'd laughed through the mess of it all. That mural stood unfinished on a warehouse wall, a promise they'd vowed to complete.

"Ray," Elias's voice cut through his reverie, low and deliberate. "You've seen what focus can do. But holding it steady, being consistent—that's the real challenge. Are you ready?"

Ray exhaled, his breath curling into the night. "I think so. What's next?"

Elias's smile was faint, edged with something unspoken. "The world doesn't test you with strangers alone. Sometimes, it's the ones who are *closest to you*, with whom you are *emotionally invested*, who push the hardest."

Before Ray could ask what he meant, the rooftop shuddered—a ripple of distortion warping the concrete beneath his feet. The skyline blurred, lights streaking into smears of colour, and then he was somewhere else. The hum of the city faded, replaced by the murmur of a crowd and the sharp tang of roasted coffee. He blinked, disoriented, finding himself in the middle of a bustling street market. Stalls lined the pavement, their holographic signs flashing deals on neural-linked gadgets and synthetic fruits. People jostled past, their voices a chaotic weave of haggling and laughter. It was his hometown, but not as he knew it—brighter, busier, a version of reality where life pulsed with a vigour he'd never dared imagine.

Elias stood beside him, arms crossed, his expression unreadable. "This is your test," he said. "Master your reaction, and you master the moment."

Ray's pulse quickened. "What am I supposed to—."

His words died as a figure pushed through the crowd, broad-shouldered and looming, his presence a dark stain against the market's vibrancy. Zane Walker. Ray's stomach twisted, the old fear clawing up his throat—a reflex from years of taunts, shoves, and smirks that had branded him as weak. But this Zane was different—older, sharper, his high school swagger hardened into something more menacing. His eyes locked onto Ray, narrowing with recognition that shouldn't exist in this shifted reality.

The Public Gauntlet

"You," Zane growled, his voice cutting through the market's din like a blade. Heads turned, a ripple of curiosity spreading through the crowd. "Still skulking around like you belong somewhere."

Ray's hands twitched, the instinct to shrink back surging like a tide. He could feel the eyes on him—dozens of strangers pausing their haggling, their faces a gallery of judgment and amusement. In 2042, he'd have ducked away, let Zane's words sink into him like poison, let the crowd's stares confirm his worthlessness. But Elias's lesson burned in his chest: *People only have power if you let them.* He'd faced Zane before, stripped him of his hold in that quiet street encounter. This was different—public, raw, a crucible of pressure meant to break him.

Zane stepped closer, his bulk casting a shadow over Ray. The crowd parted, forming a loose circle, their murmurs growing into a hum of anticipation. "What's the matter, Carter? Too scared to talk? Or just waiting for your little friend to save you again?"

The jab stung, a barb aimed at Leila's absence. Ray's jaw tightened, but he forced his breath to steady. He noticed the tremor in Zane's stance—a slight sway, a flicker of unease beneath the bravado. The Zane he'd feared had been a giant in his mind, fed by Ray's own reactions. This Zane was flesh and flaws, a man leaning on intimidation because he had nothing else. Ray saw it now: the clenched fists hiding shaky fingers, the sneer masking a hollow core.

"You don't scare me," Ray said, his voice calm but firm, loud enough to carry. The crowd hushed, the air thickening with tension. "You never did."

Zane's sneer faltered, a crack splitting his confidence. He lunged forward, shoving Ray's chest with both hands, the force enough to stagger him back a step. Gasps rippled through the onlookers, a few stepping closer as if expecting a brawl. Ray's heartbeat thundered, adrenaline urging him to swing, to shout, to give Zane the reaction he craved. But he didn't. He straightened, meeting Zane's glare with steady eyes, his hands loose at his sides.

"Is that it?" Ray asked, his tone neither mocking nor afraid—just flat, indifferent. "That's all you've got?"

Zane blinked, he was completely thrown off by the lack of fight and Ray's nonchalant demeanour. He shoved again, harder, his knuckles digging into Ray's sternum. Pain flared, but Ray didn't flinch a bit. He stood rooted, his gaze locked on Zane's, watching the bully's anger unravel into confusion. The crowd shifted, their excitement souring into discomfort. A woman muttered,

"Leave him alone," and a man turned away, bored by the one-sided spectacle.

"Fight back, damn it!" Zane snarled, his voice cracking as he grabbed Ray's jacket, yanking him forward. Their faces were inches apart, Zane's breath sour with desperation. Ray saw it then—the fear in his eyes, the need for control slipping through his fingers. This wasn't power. This was a plea of a man who was desperate to have his reaction.

"No," Ray said quietly, peeling Zane's hands off him with deliberate calm. "I don't need to."

Zane stumbled back, his chest heaving, his bravado crumbling under the weight of Ray's refusal. The crowd dispersed, their interest fading as the tension dissolved. Zane muttered a curse, his shoulders slumping, and turned away, swallowed by the market's flow. Ray exhaled, his body trembling but his mind clear. He hadn't fought— he'd won by not fighting, rather by choosing not to fight.

Elias stepped forward, a faint nod of approval in his posture. "Well done. You didn't just disarm him—you disarmed the moment."

Ray rubbed his chest, the ache a reminder of his choice. "It was harder this time. Everyone watching—it felt like they wanted me to break."

"They did," Elias said. "Pressure amplifies reaction. Mastering it in chaos is what makes you untouchable."

The Knife Of Betrayal

Before Ray could savour the victory, the market shimmered, the stalls and faces melting into shadow. The world shifted again, and he found himself in the café—their café—its warm light and coffee-scented air a stark contrast to the street's clamour. Leila sat across from him, her curly hair spilling over her shoulders, her fingers fidgeting with a folded piece of paper. She looked different here—tenser, her sharp brown eyes clouded with something Ray couldn't place. He had never seen this expression in her eyes, ever.

Guilt!

"Ray," she began, her voice soft, hesitant. "I need to tell you something."

His stomach tightened, a premonition prickling his skin. "What's wrong?"

She slid the paper across the table, her hand trembling. Ray unfolded it, his eyes scanning the text. It was an application for the EverTech internship—the one he'd dreamed of in that alternate 2038, the one he'd manifested there through belief. But the name at the top wasn't his. It was hers—*Leila Morgan*.

The words hit like a punch, stealing his breath. He'd told her about EverTech months ago, during one of their mural sessions, splashing paint and dreaming aloud about a future where he could build something real. She'd encouraged him, pushed him to apply, promised to help with the proposal. They'd even brainstormed it together— late nights over coffee, sketching ideas on napkins, laughing at his typos. It had been their project, a shared hope. And now she'd taken it.

"Why?" he managed, his voice raw, the betrayal slicing deeper than Zane's shoves.

Leila looked away, her jaw tight. "I didn't mean to hurt you. They only had one spot, and… I needed it, Ray. My family's been drowning since my brother left. I thought— I thought you'd understand."

Anger surged, hot and bitter, curling his hands into fists. The old Ray would have exploded—yelled, accused, let the wound fester into resentment. He could hear it in his head: *You stole this from me. After everything, you took it.* The café's warmth felt suffocating, the hum of other voices a distant roar. She'd been his anchor, his tether to meaning, and now she'd cut him loose.

But then Elias's words echoed: *You can't control what happens, but you can control how you react.* This was the test—the real one. Zane had been a shadow of his past; Leila was his present, her betrayal a cold blade aimed at his core. He could let it define him, let it shatter the trust they'd built, or he could choose something else. He made the choice.

He inhaled, slow and deep, forcing the anger to pass through him like smoke. He pictured the mural—their mural—its unfinished edges a testament to their bond. She'd hurt him, yes, but she wasn't the enemy. Every individual is fighting his or her own battle, so was Leila. She too was a human. She was Leila, flawed and fighting, just like him. He exhaled, the bitterness fading, replaced by a quiet resolve.

"I'm not mad," he said, surprising himself with the steadiness in his voice. "Disappointed, yeah. But mad? No, definitely not."

Leila's eyes snapped to his, wide with disbelief. "You're not?"

He shook his head, folding the paper and sliding it back to her. "What you did—it doesn't take anything from me unless I let it. I can find my own way. I always have."

Her shoulders slumped, shame flickering across her face. "I thought you'd hate me."

"Hate's a choice," Ray said, standing. "And I'm done giving it power. I am making a choice of not letting the hate define me."

He walked out, the café door chiming behind him, his heart lighter than he'd expected. The sting lingered, but it didn't own him. He'd chosen forgiveness—not for her, but for himself.

The Lesson's Depth

Elias waited outside, the night air cool against Ray's flushed skin. "You passed," he said, his tone warm but probing. "Twice over."

Ray leaned against the wall, exhaustion mingling with triumph. "That was harder than Zane. Way harder."

"It always is," Elias replied, crossing his arms. "Strangers test your surface. Those you love, with whom you are emotionally invested, test your soul. But you held steady. Why?"

Ray thought about it, the pieces clicking into place. "Because I saw it—their power over me. Zane needed me to react to feel big. Leila needed my forgiveness to feel okay. If I'd given in, I'd have lost myself, not them. My choices defined me."

Elias nodded, his eyes glinting with approval. "That's the heart of it. Life will throw chaos at you—bullies, betrayals, losses. It's not about avoiding them; it's about deciding what they mean. Most people spend their lives reacting, letting every slight dictate their days. Life keeps repeating the same lessons until you learn and people think they are unlucky. But you? You're learning to choose."

Ray looked up at the sky, the stars obscured by the city's glow. "It's not easy, though. I wanted to yell, to fight— both times. Keeping it in felt… heavy."

"That's the struggle," Elias said, stepping closer. "Non-reaction isn't weakness—it's strength refined. Like forging steel, it takes heat and pressure to make something unbreakable. You'll face worse than this, Ray—moments where the world screams for you to break. But if you can stand in that storm of fire and choose your response, nothing can touch you."

Ray let the words sink in, their weight settling over him like armour. He thought of his old life—reacting to every failure, every slight, building a prison of his own making. Now he was feeling he can never lose, he will either win or learn a lesson, either way he was a winner. Now, he saw the bars dissolving, not because the world had changed, but because he had. Zane's taunts, Leila's betrayal—they were tests, yes, but also mirrors, showing him who he could be.

"So, what now?" he asked, meeting Elias's gaze.

Elias smiled, a rare warmth softening his features. "Now, you live it. Every day's a chance to master this—to turn chaos into creation. You've got the tools. Use them."

Ray nodded, the city's hum a backdrop to his resolve. He wasn't untouchable yet—not fully—but he was closer, he was getting there. The power of non-reaction wasn't just a trick; it was a way of being, a shield against a world that thrived on breaking people down. He'd faced the market's pressure, Leila's knife, and came out stronger. Whatever came next, he'd meet it on his own terms.

The night stretched before him, alive with possibility. For the first time, he felt free—not from pain or struggle, but from their hold over him. And that, he realized, was power beyond anything he'd ever known. He knew now for sure that in life, while the pain is inevitable, the suffering is a choice. He was determined to make his choices.

Chapter - 7
Becoming, Not Getting

"Success is not about what you acquire;
it is about who you become."

— **Anonymous**

A New Lens On The World

Ray stood at the edge of the rooftop, the city sprawling beneath him like a living, breathing entity. The skyline of 2042 shimmered with artificial lights—holographic billboards pulsing with thought-responsive ads, drones weaving silently through the night air. The wind tugged at his jacket, carrying the faint hum of a world that never slept. Elias stood beside him, hands tucked into his pockets, his silver hair catching the glow of a nearby tower. The tests Ray had faced—the alternate realities, the bullies, the betrayals—had peeled back layers of illusion, leaving him raw but awake. For years, he'd chased meaning like a distant prize, something to grasp and hold. Now, he saw it differently. Meaning wasn't a finish line to cross; it was a state of being, woven into every step he took. Now he knew the meaning of life is neither given by anybody nor it is found, it is created, by choice.

"You're seeing it now, aren't you?" Elias's voice broke the silence, steady and warm, his eyes fixed on Ray with quiet expectation.

Ray nodded slowly, his breath misting in the cool air. "All this time, I thought I had to find something—purpose, happiness, some kind of success. I thought they were out there, waiting for me to catch up. But it's not about getting those things, is it? It's about who I become while I'm trying, by making my own choices."

Elias's lips curved into a small, approving smile. "Exactly. Most people spend their lives believing fulfilment lies in the next achievement—the perfect job, the right relationship, some shiny reward. They miss the truth: the journey itself is what shapes you. Perfection is a journey, not a destination. It's not about what you acquire. It's about who you become along the way. It is the process that makes you, not the result. When you do something, you become something irrespective of what you get or don't get."

The words settled over Ray like a revelation, unravelling years of restless searching. He'd always imagined life as a race to an endpoint—a place where everything would finally make sense. But standing here, with the city alive below and Elias's wisdom beside him, he realized there was no endpoint. Only the becoming. His chest felt lighter, not from certainty, but from release—the shedding of a weight he hadn't known he carried.

Living The Shift

The next morning, Ray woke to the same cracked ceiling, the same cluttered apartment, but the fog that usually clouded his mind was gone. He didn't leap out of bed with some grand plan; he simply got up, his movements deliberate and purposeful, his thoughts present and in control. For the first time, he wasn't lost in what could be or what hadn't been. He was here, in the now, and that felt like enough.

He pulled on his jacket and stepped outside, the city's pulse greeting him with its usual chaos. Hover-cars buzzed overhead, their engines a low whine against the chatter of pedestrians rushing to their routines. Ray walked among them, but he didn't feel like one of them— not anymore. Where they seemed driven by destinations, he was driven by something quieter, something internal.

Elias's lesson echoed in his skull: *It's about who you become.* He decided to test it, to live it, not as a theory but as a practice.

At the corner, a woman struggled with a spilled bag—fruits and data pads tumbling across the sidewalk, her frustration palpable as she muttered curses under her breath. The old Ray would've kept walking, head down, assuming he'd only make it worse. Today, he stopped. "Need a hand?" he asked, crouching beside her without even waiting for an answer.

She glanced up, startled, her tense expression softening. "Oh—yeah, thanks. These damn things always pick the worst time to break."

Ray gathered the scattered items—a bruised apple, a cracked data pad flashing error codes—and handed them back with a faint smile. "They've got a knack for that."

She laughed, a sharp, relieved sound, and together they repacked her bag. It took less than a minute, but as she thanked him and hurried off, Ray felt a shift—not in the world, but in himself. He hadn't fixed her day or changed her life, but he'd acted without hesitation, *without needing a reward. He had become someone who helped,* not because he had to, but because he could. The act was small, but the feeling wasn't. By choosing to help her, he felt good about himself even though he did not get anything in the worldly sense.

Later, at a corner kiosk, he bought a coffee—not his usual black, bitter brew, but something new, a spiced blend the vendor swore by. The old Ray would've stuck to routine, too afraid of disappointment to try. He was not afraid of the unfamiliar change, not anymore. Now, he sipped it, letting the unfamiliar warmth roll over his tongue. It wasn't life-changing, but it was a choice—a tiny rebellion against stagnation, against being stuck in the rut. He grinned to himself, the steam curling around his face. Becoming wasn't about grand gestures; it was about these moments, stacking one on top of another like stones in a foundation.

By noon, he found himself at the warehouse where he and Leila had started their mural months ago. The half-finished swirl of colours stared back at him, a testament to dreams paused by doubt. He'd always seen it as a failure—another thing he hadn't completed. But today, he grabbed a can of paint from the stash they'd left behind, shook it until the rattle filled the air, and sprayed a bold arc of blue across the wall. No plan, no endpoint—just movement. He understood that the stagnant water stinks while the flowing water remains fresh. The paint dripped, imperfect and alive, and Ray stepped back, hands stained, feeling not frustration but freedom. He wasn't finishing it for applause or perfection; he was painting because it felt right. Because it made him feel like someone alive.

Sara's Own Becoming

The bookstore loomed ahead, its wooden sign creaking in the breeze—a familiar refuge that now carried new weight. Ray stepped inside, the scent of old pages and roasted beans wrapping around him like a memory. Sara was there, browsing a stack of books near the back, her leather jacket slung over a chair. She didn't notice him at first, absorbed in a worn paperback, her brow furrowed in thought. Ray paused, watching her. She wasn't Leila—not the Leila of 2042—but she carried a similar fire, a spark he'd come to recognize as the mark of someone searching.

He approached, and she looked up, her sharp eyes catching his. "You look different," she said, setting the book down, her voice tinged with curiosity. "Something's changed."

Ray smirked, leaning against the shelf. "Yeah. I think I finally figured something out."

Sara tilted her head, crossing her arms. "Enlighten me."

He took a breath, choosing his words with care. "I used to think life was about getting stuff—success, happiness, love, whatever. I'd chase them like they were prizes I could win if I just tried hard enough. But now… it's not about that. It's about growing into someone who doesn't need to chase. Someone who just becomes those things naturally."

Her eyes narrowed, processing, then softened with a flicker of recognition. "So, instead of running after meaning, you focus on being it?"

"Exactly," Ray said, nodding. "I don't need to hunt it down. I just need to live in a way that makes it happen."

Sara leaned back, a thoughtful silence stretching between them. She picked up the book again, flipping it over in her hands—a collection of essays on art and rebellion. "That's… actually kind of profound," she admitted, a faint smile tugging at her lips.

Ray chuckled. "Elias would be proud."

She set the book down, her gaze drifting to the window where the city pulsed beyond the glass. "You know, I've been chasing something too. Not like you—different, but the same kind of trap."

He raised an eyebrow, inviting her to continue. She hesitated, then exhaled, her voice quieter now. "I want to make art that matters—murals, installations, something that shakes people up. But every time I start, I freeze. I keep thinking it has to be perfect, that it has to hit some big mark right away, or it's not worth doing. I've got sketches piled up in my apartment, half-finished because I'm scared they won't be enough."

Ray recognized the weight in her words—the same doubt that had shackled him for years. "What's stopping you from finishing one?"

Sara shrugged, but her eyes betrayed the truth. "Fear, I guess. That it won't mean anything. That I'll pour myself into it, and no one will care."

He nodded, understanding more than he could say. "I get that, I was there before. I used to think everything I did had to prove something—to myself, to the world. But what if it's not about proving? What if it's just about doing it because it's who you are?"

She frowned, turning the idea over in her mind. "You mean... just make it for me? Not for anyone else?"

"Yeah," Ray said, his voice steady. "Start there. Let it be yours first. If it matters to you, it'll matter to someone else eventually. But you don't have to wait for that part—you don't have to get approval to become the person who makes it."

Sara stared at him, then laughed—a soft, surprised sound. "You're starting to sound like one of those old philosophers Elias hangs around with."

"Maybe I am," Ray grinned. "But it's working for me. Try it—pick one sketch, finish it. Not for a gallery, not for a crowd. Just for you."

She picked up the book again, clutching it like a lifeline. "Okay. One sketch. I've got this idea—a mural of hands breaking through walls, all colours crashing together. Been sitting on it for weeks."

"Sounds like it's ready to get out," Ray said. "Let it."

Sara nodded, a spark igniting in her eyes—a mirror of the fire he'd felt growing in himself. "You're not as lost as you used to be, you know that?"

"I'm getting there," he replied, and for the first time, he believed it.

The Joy Of The Journey

That evening, Ray returned to the rooftop, the city's glow painting the sky in shades of amber and steel. Elias was already there, leaning against the railing, his silhouette a quiet constant in Ray's shifting world. The air carried a chill, but Ray felt warm, alive with a clarity he hadn't known before.

"So," Elias said, turning to face him, "what do you think?"

Ray joined him at the railing, the cool metal grounding him as he looked out over the buildings. "I think I get it now. You didn't tell me what to do—you gave me chances to figure it out myself. The tests, the shifts—they weren't about finding answers. They were about seeing things differently, having different perspectives."

Elias smiled, a rare warmth softening his features. "If you help a butterfly, struggling to come out of the cocoon, by breaking the cocoon then actually you are not helping it. If you do that the butterfly will never develop the strength to fly of its own, it will die there without ever being able to fly. The struggle that butterfly does while coming out of the cocoon is giving it strength. That's how it works. Real learning isn't handed to you—it's something you wrestle with, something you claim. I could've told you the truth from the start, but would you have believed it?"

"No," Ray admitted, his voice quiet but sure. "I had to live it, experience it."

"And you did," Elias said, his eyes glinting with approval. "You're not the same kid who climbed up here looking for a way out. You've become something more. The question is—what now?"

Ray thought about the day—the woman with the bag, the coffee, the mural, Sara's spark. Small moments, but each one a thread in a tapestry he was weaving, *not for some distant reward*, but for the joy of the weaving itself. "I used to think I needed a plan," he said, "a map to tell me where I was going. But now… I don't need to know the whole road. Just the next step. Life is like a mountain road, while driving, you don't see the entire road from the beginning till the end. You see the road only up to the next turn, and, when you reach that turn you see further till the next turn. Despite not knowing what lies after the next turn, you keep going."

Elias nodded, his gaze drifting to the horizon. "That's the beauty of it. People chase destinations, thinking that's where happiness lives. They miss the part where the process—the becoming—is the real joy. Every choice, every moment you're present for, that's what builds you."

Ray's chest tightened, not with pressure, but with possibility. "It's not always easy, though. Today felt good—helping someone, painting, talking to Sara. But what about the days it doesn't? When it's messy or hard?"

"Then you lean into the mess," Elias said, his tone firm but kind. "The hard days are where you grow the most, you become something. Joy isn't the absence of struggle—it's finding something worth it in the middle of it. You don't get stronger by avoiding the weight; you get stronger by lifting it."

Ray let the words sink in, picturing the mural's dripping paint, Sara's unfinished sketches, his own shaky steps forward. "So, it's about showing up even when every pore of your body tells you not to," he said, half to himself. "Even when it's not perfect. *You cannot always be the best*, but, *you can always be at your best* Ray."

"Especially then," Elias replied. "Perfection's a myth—it's just a trap to keep you waiting, to stagnate. Becoming's about movement, not arrival."

A slow smile spread across Ray's face, the city's hum a backdrop to his resolve. "Guess I'll find out what that looks like."

Elias clapped a hand on his shoulder, the gesture solid and steady. "You already are. Keep going, Ray. The joy's in the doing."

Ray took a deep breath, the air sharp and alive against his skin. He'd spent so long searching for meaning outside himself, only to find it was something he carried—something he built with every choice he made, every act of presence. He didn't need to know the whole path; he just needed to walk it, one step at a time, becoming more with each one irrespective of material gain.

The city stretched before him, a sea of lights and shadows, a world he was no longer afraid to shape. For the first time, he felt ready—not for some grand finale, but for the quiet, steady work of becoming. And that, he realized, was more than enough.

Chapter - 8
A Life That Matters

"It is not the length of life, but the depth of life."

— **Ralph Waldo Emerson**

The Rooftop Revelation

Ray stood on the familiar rooftop, the city of 2042 sprawling beneath him like a restless sea of light and shadow. The air was sharp with the tang of metal and exhaust, carried on a breeze that tugged at his worn jacket. The skyline shimmered with holographic billboards—thought-responsive ads flickering with *promises of instant gratification*—and the distant hum of drones wove a constant thread through the night. It was a world he'd once seen as a prison, its routines and expectations chaining him to a life of quiet despair. But now, as he gazed out over it, he saw something else: a canvas, vast and uncharted, waiting for him to decide what mark he'd leave.

Elias stood beside him, his silver hair catching the glow of a nearby tower, his presence a quiet anchor in the storm of Ray's thoughts. The lessons—the shifts in reality, the tests of perception, the battles with his own doubts and fears—had stripped away the illusions he'd clung to. He'd spent years believing life was a puzzle to be solved, a riddle with an answer he'd never find. But it wasn't. *It was a process*, process which makes you, a journey, not a destination, and he held the brush to paint it. For the first time, he asked himself a question that wasn't about escaping but about creating: *What kind of life do I want to live?*

The answer came not as a list of goals—wealth, fame, comfort—but as a feeling, deep and resonant. *He didn't want a life measured by years or accolades.* He wanted one that mattered, one that rippled outward, touching others as Elias had touched him. He wanted to live for a cause, not for applause. He turned to the older man, his voice steady despite the weight of the moment. "I see it now. Life isn't about solving something—it's about building something, and, in the process, you become something."

Elias's eyes glinted with approval, though his expression remained measured. "And what will you build, Ray?"

Ray exhaled, his breath curling into the cool air. "Something real. Something that helps people wake up— like you did for me."

A faint smile tugged at Elias's lips. "Then you're ready for the final lesson."

Two Futures, Two Paths

Before Ray could ask what he meant, the rooftop shuddered, the concrete beneath his feet rippling like water disturbed by a stone. The skyline blurred, lights streaking into smears of colour, and a wave of dizziness gripped him. He closed his eyes instinctively, steadying himself against the railing, and when he opened them, the world had shifted.

He stood in a luxurious apartment, its floor-to-ceiling windows offering a panoramic view of a pristine, orderly city. The air smelled faintly of lavender and polished wood, a stark contrast to the gritty chaos of 2042. The space was immaculate—white furniture, sleek tech embedded in every surface, a holographic display cycling through news feeds and stock prices. Ray moved through it, his footsteps silent on the plush carpet, a strange detachment settling over him. This wasn't his apartment—not the cluttered, cracked-ceiling mess he called home—but unsurprisingly, it felt familiar, as if he belonged here.

A mirror caught his eye, and he froze. The reflection staring back was him, but older—mid-thirties, perhaps—his hair neatly trimmed, his dark eyes sharp but cold. He wore a tailored suit, a gold watch glinting on his wrist, and carried himself with the effortless confidence of someone who'd won the life's game. Papers on a nearby desk confirmed it: *Ryan Carter, Senior VP, EverTech.* A flood of images rushed through his mind—memories that weren't his, yet felt real. Years of climbing corporate ladders, sealing deals, amassing wealth. A life of affluence and comfort, of predictability, where every need was effortlessly met, every risk was meticulously avoided.

He wandered to the window, gazing out at the city below. It was pristine, yes, but sterile—people moved like automatons, their faces blank, their lives dictated by routine. No chaos, no struggle, no depth. He saw himself in boardrooms, sipping expensive scotch at galas, retiring to this silent penthouse night after night. Alone. The wealth was there, the status undeniable, but it was hollow and shallow—a life of getting everything, but not becoming. A shiver ran through him, not from cold, but from the realization that this could have been his future. A safe path, a predictable one, where he'd traded his fire for comfort.

The world shifted again, the apartment dissolving into darkness, then re-forming into something entirely different. Ray stumbled, catching himself on a rickety table in a cramped, dimly lit room. The air was thick with the scent of paint and coffee, the walls plastered with sketches, notes, and photographs. A battered laptop glowed on a desk cluttered with books and half-empty mugs. Outside, the city was louder, messier—2042 as he knew it, but alive with a vibrancy he hadn't noticed before.

He glanced at his reflection in a cracked mirror—still him, still older, but different. His hair was longer, streaked with grey, his face lined with the wear of effort, not ease. His clothes were worn but practical, stained with paint and ink. The desk held a stack of letters, some scrawled in hurried handwriting: *"Your book changed my life," "I started my own project because of you."* A memory flashed—standing before a crowd of young faces, speaking words that sparked hope, guiding them to see their own power. This wasn't a life of wealth; it was a life of impact—of chaos, yes, but a chaos that birthed change.

He stepped to the window, peering out at a street alive with movement—people arguing, laughing, building. Murals splashed colour across grey walls, remnants of a project he'd started with Leila years ago. He saw himself in this future too—tired, often uncertain, but never alone. Friends, mentees, a community of seekers surrounded him, their lives interwoven with his life meaningfully. It wasn't perfect but satisfying. Bills piled up, doubts lingered, but every struggle carried meaning, helped him become something. Every moment was a brushstroke on a canvas that stretched beyond himself.

The rooftop snapped back into focus, the visions fading like smoke. Ray's knees trembled, his breath ragged as he gripped the railing. Two futures—one of shallow comfort, the other one thought messy but was having a deep and meaningful purpose. Elias watched him, silent, waiting.

"I could've had that first life," Ray said, his voice hoarse. "Safe. Easy. But it wouldn't have mattered to me or anyone at the end."

And this one?" Elias prompted, his tone neutral but probing.

Ray straightened, the fire in his chest flaring. "This one does. It's harder, messier, but it's real, having meaning and purpose. It's about impact—about helping people see what I've seen. Not just existing, but living."

Elias nodded, a slow, deliberate gesture. "Then you've chosen."

The First Step Forward

The weight of that choice settled over Ray, heavy but exhilarating. He didn't want to drift through life anymore, a spectator to his own existence. He wanted to act, to create, to leave something behind that echoed beyond his years. But, *knowing what he wanted wasn't enough—he had to start somewhere.*

The next day, he walked the city streets with new eyes, the hum of 2042 wrapping around him like a call to action. He passed a community centre, its faded sign advertising a youth mentorship program. The old Ray would've kept walking, dismissing it as someone else's problem. But now, he stopped, peering through the grimy window at a group of teens huddled around a table, their faces a mix of boredom and defiance. He saw himself in them—lost, searching, unsure if anything mattered.

He pushed open the door, the bell jangling overhead. A woman with tired eyes and a clipboard glanced up from the counter. "Can I help you?"

"I'm here about the mentorship thing," Ray said, surprising himself with the steadiness in his voice. "I want to get involved."

She raised an eyebrow, sizing him up. "You got experience with kids?"

"Not really," he admitted, shifting his weight. "But I've got something to say. I think I can reach them, help them."

She studied him for a moment, then handed him a form. "We're short-staffed. If you're serious, we'll take you. First session's tomorrow—be here at three."

Ray nodded, clutching the paper like a lifeline. As he left, a kid slouched against the wall outside caught his eye— fourteen, maybe, with a mop of dark hair and a scowl that screamed defiance. Their gazes locked, and Ray felt a jolt of recognition. This was his chance—his first mentee, whether the kid knew it or not.

"Hey," Ray called, stepping closer. "What's your name?"

The kid glared, kicking at the pavement. "Why do you care?"

"Because I've been where you are," Ray said, keeping his tone even. "Stuck. Thinking nothing matters. I'm Ray."

The kid hesitated, then muttered, "Kai."

"Kai," Ray repeated, nodding. "You ever feel like the world's just waiting for you to screw up?"

Kai's scowl faltered, a flicker of surprise breaking through. "Yeah. All the time."

"Me too," Ray said. "But it doesn't have to be that way. Stick around tomorrow—I've got a story you might want to hear."

Kai shrugged, but his eyes lingered on Ray, curiosity warring with mistrust. "Maybe."

Ray grinned, turning away. "See you then."

It wasn't much—a name, a spark—but it was a start. He could feel it: the ripple beginning, the first brushstroke on a canvas he'd only just begun to imagine.

Elias's Challenge

That night, Ray returned to the rooftop, the city's glow painting the sky in shades of amber and steel. Elias was already there, leaning against the railing, his silhouette a constant in Ray's shifting world. The air carried a chill, but Ray felt warm, alive with immense possibilities.

"You've started," Elias said, his voice cutting through the quiet. "The mentorship. The kid."

Ray nodded, leaning beside him. "Yeah. It's small, but it feels right."

Elias turned, his sharp eyes boring into Ray's. "Small's a start, but it's not enough. You've seen what's possible—two futures, two lives. You've picked the harder one. Now you have to commit to it."

Ray frowned, the intensity in Elias's tone catching him off guard. "I am committed. I'm not going back to the old me."

"Are you sure?" Elias pressed, stepping closer. "It's easy to dip your toes in, to play at purpose when it feels good. But what about when it doesn't? When the kid doesn't show up? When the world pushes back? *Commitment isn't a feeling*, Ray—*it's a choice you make every day, even when it hurts*."

Ray's stomach tightened, the weight of Elias's words sinking in. He thought of Kai's guarded eyes, the uncertainty in his own steps. "I want this," he said, his voice firm but edged with doubt. "I want to make a difference."

"Then prove it," Elias challenged, his tone unyielding. "Don't just help one kid—build something bigger. Write what you've learned, share it, wake people up. The enforcers are watching—they've been watching since you stepped through that door. They'll come for you when you're a threat. You think they'll let you change the game without a fight?"

Ray's pulse quickened, a chill prickling his skin. "The enforcers?"

Elias's gaze darkened. "You've felt them—the hum, the shadows. They keep this world predictable, controllable. You're a glitch now, Ray. A variable they can't account for. Choose this life fully, and they'll notice. Half measures won't protect you—or anyone else."

Ray swallowed, the stakes sharpening into focus. He'd sensed it—the faint vibrations, the fleeting glimpses of something watching. He'd brushed it off as paranoia, but Elias's warning made it real. This wasn't just about him anymore; it was about what he could ignite, what he could defend.

"I'm not afraid," Ray said, meeting Elias's gaze. "I'll do it—all of it. The mentorship, the writing, whatever it takes. Not for me, but for them."

Elias studied him, then nodded, a rare warmth breaking through his sternness. "Good. Because *it's not enough to choose a life that matters—you have to live it. Every day. No excuses.*"

Ray clenched his fists, resolve hardening within him. "No excuses."

Elias stepped back, his silhouette blending into the night. "Then get to work. The world's waiting."

Ray turned to the city, its lights stretching out like a challenge. He thought of Kai, of the countless others like him—lost, searching, ready to be found. He thought of the safe future he'd rejected, its hollow comfort fading into irrelevance. This path was harder, riskier, but it was his. He'd write, he'd mentor, he'd fight—not for applause, but the cause, for the depth, for the impact, for a life that reverberated beyond himself.

The hum pulsed faintly in the distance, a whisper of what was to come. Ray squared his shoulders, unafraid. Let them watch. Let them try. He'd chosen his canvas, picked up his brush, and he wouldn't stop painting—not now, not ever, come what may.

Chapter - 9
The Last Reality Shift

The Threshold Of Doubt

Ray stood before the rusted rooftop door, its surface pitted and scarred by years of neglect. The city of this alternate 2038 hummed below, its golden light spilling across the skyline, a deceptive glow that masked the strangeness of a life he hadn't lived. The key Elias had given him weighed heavy in his pocket, its edges pressing against his palm as if urging him to act. His breath came in shallow bursts, fogging in the cool night air, each exhale a battle against the tide of uncertainty crashing within him. He'd crossed this threshold once before—stepped through into a world where he was *Ryan*, not Ray—and now, he had to choose whether to cross it again, to reclaim the reality he'd left behind.

The door loomed like a sentinel, its silence louder than the city's distant roar. Ray's hand hovered over the keyhole, trembling not from cold but from the storm of doubt raging in his mind. What if he couldn't go back? What if this was his reality now—a life of bold choices and unearned triumphs, a life that wasn't truly his? The thought clawed at him, dragging up memories of failures he'd buried deep—moments when he'd stood at the edge of possibility and turned away, letting fear paint his world grey.

He saw himself at sixteen, hunched over a desk in his childhood bedroom, the college application to EverTech open on his cracked screen. His fingers had hovered over the submit button, heart pounding with a mix of hope and dread, but the voice in his head—his own voice—had whispered, *you'll fail. They'll see right through you.* He'd closed the tab, deleted the draft, and watched the opportunity slip away, convincing himself it didn't matter. The memory stung, sharp and vivid, a reminder of the Ray who'd expected nothing and gotten exactly that.

Another vision flickered—eighteen, a rainy night at the edge of town, a girl with bright eyes and a laugh that cut through his gloom. She'd asked him to come with her, to leave the city for a weekend of music and freedom, but he'd hesitated. *What if I ruin it? What if she realizes I'm not enough?* He'd stayed behind, watching her taillights fade into the storm, the silence of his apartment swallowing him whole. That was the Ray who'd let life slip through his fingers, who'd built a prison of his own making.

And then the rooftop—two years ago, before this journey began. He'd stood at the ledge, the wind biting his face, staring down at the abyss not because he wanted to die, but because he didn't know how to live. Leila had pulled him back, her presence a lifeline he hadn't deserved, but even then, he'd doubted. *Why me? Why does she bother?* He'd let her faith in him be a crutch, not a catalyst, wallowing in apathy while she fought for them both, alone.

The visions pressed against him, a gallery of failures threatening to drown him in their weight. His hand dropped from the keyhole, his chest tightening as the old Ray—the one who'd never dared—clawed to the surface. What if this door led nowhere? What if Elias had lied, and 2042 was gone, leaving him stranded in a reality that didn't fit? The hum of the city below sharpened, a mocking chorus to his indecision.

But then another sound cut through—a steady tap of boots on concrete. Leila—no, Sara—emerged from the stairwell, her leather jacket catching the light, her sharp eyes narrowing as they found him. She stopped a few paces away, arms crossed, her presence a jolt that steadied his spiralling thoughts. "You're not bailing on me now, are you?" she said, her voice light but laced with a challenge.

Ray turned to her, the visions receding like shadows before a flame. "I don't know if I can do this," he admitted, his voice raw. "What if I'm wrong? What if I step through, and it's just… nothing?"

Sara's brow furrowed, but she didn't flinch. "You've been saying 'what if' since I met you—or whoever you think I am here. But you're still standing there, holding that key. That's not nothing."

Her words pierced him, a lifeline pulling him from the undertow of doubt. She wasn't his Leila—not exactly— but she carried the same fire, the same unyielding belief that had saved him before. He gripped the cold key tighter, its edges biting into his skin, grounding him in the moment. "I've messed up so many times," he said, quieter now. "Back home—back in my world—I let everything pass me by. What if I'm just running from that again?"

Sara stepped closer, her gaze unflinching. "Then stop running. You're not that guy anymore—I can see it. Whatever you've been through, it's changed you. So, quit doubting and choose. That door's not going to wait forever."

Her certainty anchored him, a mirror reflecting the man he'd become, not the boy he'd been. The visions of failure lingered, but they no longer owned him. He'd faced Zane without reacting, forgiven Leila's betrayal, rewritten reality with his belief. Each stumble had built him, not broken him. Elias's voice echoed in his skull: *Your world is the result of what you focus on.* He could focus on the past—on the failures that had defined him—or he could focus on the now, on the choice before him.

Ray exhaled, slow and deliberate, the tension draining from his shoulders. "Okay," he said, meeting her eyes. "Together?"

Sara grinned, a spark of mischief lighting her face. "Always."

Leila As Anchor

He slid the key into the lock, the metal scraping against rust with a sound that reverberated through the night. The door pulsed faintly, a warm rush of energy spilling out as it had before, prickling his skin and humming in his bones. Sara's hand brushed his arm, a steadying touch that reminded him he wasn't alone—not here, not now. The light flared, searing his vision white, and his stomach lurched as reality tilted beneath him.

When the world steadied, he was back—the rooftop of 2042 stretching before him, the city's artificial glow painting the sky in shades of amber and steel. The air carried the familiar tang of exhaust, the hum of drones threading through the night. Relief flooded him, sharp and sweet, but it was tempered by a flicker of loss. The 2038 Sara was gone, a fragment of a life he'd briefly claimed. He turned, expecting to see her beside him, but it was Leila—his Leila—standing there, her curly hair spilling over her shoulders, her sharp brown eyes wide with a mix of awe and confusion.

"Ray?" she said, her voice trembling but firm. "What the hell just happened?"

He laughed, a raw, unsteady sound that broke the silence. "We're back. It worked."

Leila stepped closer, her gaze darting from him to the door, then back again. "Back? Where were we? One minute we're here, then there's this light, and now—" She stopped, her hands balling into fists as if to anchor herself. "You're going explain this, right?"

Ray nodded, his mind racing to piece it together for her—for himself. "It was another reality. 2038. A version of us—of me—that made different choices. Elias sent us there, and I… I had to figure out how to get back."

Her eyes narrowed, but there was no disbelief, only a fierce curiosity he knew too well. "And you did. How?"

"I chose it," he said, the simplicity of it striking him anew. "I stopped doubting and decided this is where I belong. With you."

Leila's expression softened, a rare vulnerability breaking through her storm of purpose. "You're an idiot, you know that? Dragging me into some cosmic mess without a heads-up."

He smirked, the tension easing between them. "You dragged me off this rooftop first. Call it even?"

She laughed, a sharp, bright sound that cut through the night, and punched his arm lightly. "Fine. But you owe me coffee—and a damn good story."

Her presence steadied him, a tether to the world he'd fought to reclaim. She didn't know the full scope of what he'd seen—the alternate lives, the tests, the power he'd tapped into—but she didn't need to. Not yet. She was here, real and unshaken, the anchor that had pulled him through every shift. He thought of the mural they'd started, its unfinished edges waiting below—a promise they'd keep together, no matter what realities lay beyond.

Elias's Farewell

Footsteps echoed from the stairwell, deliberate and slow. Ray tensed, his hand drifting to his pocket where the key still rested, but relief washed over him as Elias emerged from the shadows. His silver hair glinted under the city's glow, his eyes sharp with a mix of pride and something darker—something unresolved.

"You did it," Elias said, his voice warm but edged with a weight Ray couldn't place. "You chose your reality."

Ray nodded, stepping forward. "Yeah. But it wasn't easy. I almost didn't make it."

Elias's smile was faint, tinged with a sadness Ray hadn't seen before. "That's why it matters. The hardest choices are the ones that define us."

Leila crossed her arms, eyeing Elias with the same suspicion she'd shown in the bookstore. "So, what now? You keep throwing us through doors until we figure out the universe?"

Elias chuckled, a low sound that carried more weariness than humour. "No, Leila. This was the last shift—for now. Ray's proven what he needed to. The rest is up to him."

Ray frowned, the words sinking in. "For now? What does that mean?"

Elias stepped closer, his gaze piercing through the night. "You've seen the edges of what's possible, Ray. You've bent reality to your will. But there's more out there— more than I can show you. The world you've reclaimed isn't the only one watching."

A chill prickled Ray's skin, the memory of Elias's earlier warning resurfacing. *They watch. They enforce.* "The enforcers," he said, his voice low. "You're talking about them."

Elias's expression darkened, a shadow passing over his features. "Among others. You've tugged at their threads, and they don't like loose ends. But you're not alone—they can't touch what you've built unless you let them."

Ray's chest tightened, the hum of the city sharpening at the edges of his senses. "You're leaving, aren't you?"

Elias didn't answer directly, his silence a confirmation heavier than words. He reached into his coat, pulling out a small, worn notebook—its pages yellowed, its cover scarred—and pressed it into Ray's hands. "Keep asking questions," he said. "Keep choosing. This isn't the end—it's a beginning I won't be here to see."

Ray gripped the notebook, its weight a promise and a burden. "Where are you going?"

Elias's eyes flickered to the horizon, where the first hints of dawn glowed faintly. "Somewhere I'm needed. You don't need me anymore—not like you did. But if you listen, you'll hear me in the quiet."

He stepped back, his silhouette blending into the shadows, but his final words lingered, cryptic and heavy. "Beware the ones who guard the frame, Ray. They'll test you again—when you least expect it."

And then he was gone, the stairwell swallowing him whole, leaving only the echo of his steps. Ray stared after him, the notebook warm against his palm, a thousand questions burning in his throat. The enforcers, the frame—what did it mean? What lay beyond this reality he'd claimed? The hum pulsed faintly, a whisper of something watching, waiting. But it didn't scare him—not anymore.

Leila nudged him, her voice pulling him back. "He's a weird one. You okay?"

Ray exhaled, tucking the notebook into his jacket. "Yeah. I think so."

She nodded, her grin returning. "Good. Because we've got a mural to finish—and a whole lot of coffee to drink."

He laughed, the sound grounding him in the now. The rooftop stretched silent around them, the city alive below.

Elias was gone, but his lessons remained—etched into Ray's mind, his choices, his reality. The last shift was

over, but the dance wasn't. Whatever came next—the enforcers, the mysteries, the threads of a larger tapestry—he'd face it on his terms, with Leila at his side.

Ray turned from the door, the key a quiet weight in his pocket. The dawn crept closer, a new light for a world he'd chosen. And for the first time, he was definitively ready to join it.

Chapter - 10
Leap Of Belief

"Belief is not a hope—it's a force. What you hold true bends the entire world to meet it."

— **Anonymous**

The Edge Of Everything

Ray stood at the rooftop's edge, the city of 2042 sprawling beneath him like a restless beast, its veins of light pulsing against the bruised night sky. The wind whipped through his messy black hair, tugging at his jacket, a cold reminder of the height, the fall, the choice he faced. His boots grazed the concrete lip, pebbles skittering into the abyss below—a sound swallowed by the distant hum of drones and the murmur of lives he'd once envied for their certainty. The key from Elias's book rested heavy in his pocket, its edges worn smooth by his restless fingers, a silent promise he wasn't sure he could keep.

Leila stood a few paces behind, her curly hair loose in the breeze, her sharp brown eyes fixed on him with an intensity that made his chest ache. She didn't speak—not yet—but her presence was a tether, grounding him as his mind constantly teetered between doubt and daring. The rooftop wasn't just a place tonight; it was a threshold, a line between the Ray who'd drifted through life and the Ray who might—might—step into something more.

He'd returned here after the last shift, after choosing 2042 over the alternate 2038, after Elias's cryptic farewell had left him with more questions than answers, like always. The notebook Elias had given him sat tucked inside his jacket, its pages unopened but buzzing with a weight he couldn't ignore. He'd thought returning to his reality would bring clarity, a sense of home. Instead, it brought this—a gnawing pull to act, to test the limits of what he'd learned, to leap not just through doors but into the unknown itself.

His breath hitched, fogging in the frigid air. Below, the alley waited, a shadowed maw that promised either oblivion or revelation. He'd leapt before—through the rusted door, into a life that wasn't his—but that had been carefully guided, orchestrated by Elias's hand. This was different. *This was his choice*, unprompted, unwritten. There were no guarantees. The thought tightened his throat, a cocktail of fear and exhilaration he couldn't swallow down.

"You're thinking too much," Leila said, her voice cutting through the wind like a blade. She stepped closer, her boots scuffing the concrete, her arms crossed not in judgment but in challenge. "You've been staring at that drop for ten minutes. What's stopping you?"

Ray turned to her, his dark eyes meeting hers, searching for the certainty she always seemed to carry. "What if I'm wrong?" he said, his voice raw, quieter than he'd meant it to be. "What if I jump, and it's just… nothing? No shift, no lesson, just a fall?"

Leila's lips pressed into a thin line, her gaze softening but unwavering. "And what if you don't jump, Ray? What if you stay here, stuck, wondering forever? You've already come this far—don't tell me you're going let fear win now."

Her words stung, not because they were harsh, but because they were true. *He'd spent years letting fear dictate his steps—fear of failure, of rejection, of being less than he could be.* It had kept him small, invisible, a shadow in his own life. But the shifts, the tests, Elias's lessons—they'd cracked that shell, let light seep into the places he'd kept dark. He wasn't that Ray anymore. Or he didn't have to be.

"I don't know what's down there," he admitted, his hands trembling as he gripped the railing. "What if I can't control it? What if I lose everything I've figured out?"

Leila stepped beside him, her shoulder brushing his, a quiet solidarity that steadied his racing heart. "You won't lose it," she said, her tone softer now, laced with something deeper—something personal. "You've got me here, don't you? And I'm not letting you fall apart—not after all this." It wasn't just an assurance, it felt like unconditional commitment.

Leila's Heart

Ray glanced at her, caught off guard by the vulnerability in her voice. Leila was a storm, a force of purpose that swept him along when he couldn't move himself. But now, standing here, he saw more—the cracks beneath her resolve, the weight she carried that she rarely let show.

"Why do you keep doing this?" he asked, the question spilling out before he could stop it. "Pushing me, dragging me out of my head—why does it matter to you?"

She looked away, her gaze drifting to the city below, her fingers tightening around her arms. For a moment, he thought she wouldn't answer. Then she exhaled, a shaky breath that carried years of unspoken pain. "Because I couldn't save him," she said, her voice barely above a whisper. "My brother—Evan. He was like you, Ray. Lost, doubting, thinking nothing mattered. I tried to pull him out, but I was too late. He jumped—not off a roof, but into something he couldn't come back from. Drugs, despair, whatever you want to call it. I found him one morning, and he was just… gone."

Ray's chest tightened, a lump rising in his throat. He'd never known—never asked. All those nights she'd hauled him to the bookstore, forced him to face the world, he'd assumed it was her stubbornness, her need to fix things. But it was more. It was grief, turned into a vow. Bad experiences make some people bitter, some become better. She didn't let that bad experience make her bitter, she got better. She had made a choice.

"I didn't see it then," she continued, her eyes glistening but fierce. "How much he needed someone to believe in him when he couldn't. So, when I found you up here two years ago, I promised myself that I wouldn't let it happen again, no matter what. Ray, you're not Evan, but, you've got that same spark that he lost. I won't watch it fade—not if I can help it."

Her words hit him like a wave, washing away the last threads of doubt clinging to his resolve. She wasn't just his anchor—she was his mirror, reflecting a strength he hadn't claimed until now. He reached out, resting a hand on her shoulder, a silent promise in the gesture, a reciprocal commitment. "I'm not going anywhere," he said. "Not like that."

She nodded, a small, relieved smile breaking through. "Good. Then leap, you idiot. Show me what you've got."

Fear And Hope

Ray turned back to the edge, the city's lights blurring into a sea of possibility below. Fear gnawed at him—vivid, visceral, painting images of twisted limbs and shattered dreams. He saw himself falling, crashing into the alley, his body broken on the unforgiving pavement, the key useless in his pocket. He saw the enforcers Elias had warned of—those shadowy watchers—laughing from the void, proving his belief was a delusion, his power a lie. Failure loomed, a spectre he'd known too well, whispering that he'd never been enough.

But then hope flickered—a brighter, fiercer flame. What if he didn't fall? What if he leapt and the world bent to meet him, as it had through the door? He pictured landing—not broken, but whole—his feet hitting the ground with a force that rippled outward, reshaping the alley, the city, the reality he claimed as his own. He saw himself not as a victim of gravity, but as its master, the belief carrying him where doubt never could. Elias's voice echoed: *Your thoughts are more powerful than you realize.* He'd rewritten coffee cups, faced bullies, chosen his world. Why not this?

The two visions battled within him—failure's cold grip versus transformation's warm pull. His breath steadied, his hands unclenching as he let fear pass through him, not over him. He wasn't leaping blind. He was leaping with intent, with faith in what he'd become. The key in his pocket wasn't just metal—it was a symbol of his power, his choice. He didn't need Elias to guide him this time. He'd guide himself.

"Okay," he said, more to himself than Leila. "Let's see what happens."

Elias's Echo

As if summoned by the thought, footsteps echoed from the stairwell—slow, deliberate, a rhythm Ray knew too well. Elias emerged from the shadows, his silver hair glinting under the faint glow of a rooftop bulb, his eyes sharp with a mix of curiosity and expectation. He stopped a few feet away, hands in his pockets, his presence a quiet challenge.

"You're here," Ray said, surprise mingling with relief.

Elias tilted his head, a faint smirk tugging at his lips. "Did you think I'd miss this?"

Ray swallowed, the weight of Elias's gaze pushing him to speak. "I don't know if I can do it. Leap, I mean. Not through a door, but… just me."

Elias stepped closer, his voice low but resonant, cutting through the wind. "You've already done it, Ray. Every shift, every test—it's been you leaping, even when you didn't see it. The door was just a tool. The real power's here." He tapped his temple, his eyes firmly locking onto Ray's. "Reality's fluid—it bends to what you hold true. I learned that the hard way."

Ray frowned, catching the shift in Elias's tone. "What do you mean?"

Elias's gaze drifted to the horizon, a shadow passing over his face. "Years ago, I stood where you are—on a rooftop, not this one, but close enough. I'd lost everything—

family, purpose—because I believed the world was fixed, unchangeable. I leapt, expecting to end it. But I didn't fall. I landed somewhere else—another reality, one I'd shaped without knowing. It terrified me, but it taught me: belief isn't passive. It's a force. I've been running from that truth ever since, guiding others to face it instead. You're the first who's come this far."

Ray's breath caught, the story sinking in. Elias wasn't just a mentor—he was a survivor, a man who'd leapt and lived, who'd seen the edges of what Ray was only beginning to grasp. "So, this works?" he asked, his voice steadier now. "If I believe it?"

Elias nodded, his smirk softening into something warmer. "It always has. The question is what you believe, *how strongly you believe*—failure, or something more?"

Ray looked back at the edge, Elias's words igniting the hope he'd clung to. He saw it now—the leap wasn't about the fall; it was about the landing. About choosing what came next. He pulled the key from his pocket, holding it up to the light, its surface catching the city's glow. "Something more," he said in a definitive and decisive manner, slipping it back into his jacket.

Elias stepped back, giving him space. "Then show me."

The Leap

Ray faced the drop, his heart pounding but his mind clear. Leila's hand brushed his arm, a final nudge of faith. "You've got this," she whispered, her voice a lifeline he didn't need to clutch—just knowing it was there was enough.

He took a breath, deep and deliberate, letting the city's hum fill him. Fear lingered, a faint echo, but hope drowned it out. He didn't need to know the outcome— only that *his belief in himself will shape it*. His legs tensed, his body coiling with intent, and then he leapt.

The wind roared past, a howl that swallowed his gasp as the rooftop vanished above him. His stomach flipped, the alley rushing up to meet him, but he didn't flinch, not a bit. He focused—on landing, on bending the fall to his will. The air thickened, resisting gravity's pull, and then his boots hit the ground—not with a crash, but with a soft thud, the pavement rippling faintly beneath him like water settling after a stone's drop.

He stood, unharmed, adrenaline surging through him as he looked up. Leila leaned over the edge, her grin wide and triumphant, Elias beside her, his nod conveyed a silent approval. The alley stretched around him, solid and real, but alive with a possibility he'd summoned.

Ray laughed—a raw, exultant sound that echoed off the walls. He'd leapt, not through a door, but through belief itself. The city loomed above, waiting for his next move. He didn't know what lay ahead—the enforcers, the mysteries Elias hinted at—but he knew one thing: he was ready.

The hum pulsed faintly, a whisper of what might come. Ray squared his shoulders, grinning into the night. Let them watch. He was determined to bend the world again—and again—and again— until it matched the man he wanted to become.

Chapter - 11
The Unseen Framework

"The world doesn't hide its secrets—it reveals them to those who dare to look."

— Anonymous

A Spark Ignites

Ray pushed open the chipped wooden door of the community centre, the hinges creaking like a reluctant confession. Inside, the air hung heavy with the scent of stale coffee and damp concrete, a stark contrast to the sterile hum of 2042's city streets beyond the grimy windows. The room buzzed with a restless energy—teens sprawled across mismatched chairs, their voices a low murmur of defiance and boredom, their thumbs flicking over phone screens or drumming against scarred table tops. It was a chaos Ray recognized, a mirror of the turmoil he'd carried at their age—lost, searching, unsure if anything mattered.

He slid into a seat at a battered table near the back, his notebook thudding softly against the wood as he set it down. Its pages were a mess of ink—scribbled thoughts from the rooftop leap two nights ago, fragments of Elias's lessons, questions he hadn't yet answered. His fingers traced the worn cover, grounding him as he scanned the room. These kids weren't so different from him—trapped in a world that demanded conformity, their dreams buried under the weight of silent expectations of societal norms. He'd come here to change that, to plant a spark where he'd once let apathy reign.

Across from him sat Kai, the boy he'd met outside the centre the day before. Fourteen, lean as a wire, with dark hair spilling into his eyes and a scowl that seemed carved into his face. His sneakers kicked a steady rhythm against the table leg, a restless pulse that matched the tension in his hunched shoulders. In his hands, he clutched a sketchpad, its edges crumpled and torn—less from carelessness, Ray suspected, and more from the battles it had survived. Kai didn't look up, his focus pinned to the paper as if it were a shield against the world.

Ray leaned forward, keeping his voice low but deliberate. "So, you said you won't stick around. Why'd you come back?"

Kai shrugged, a half-hearted twitch of his shoulders, his eyes still glued to the sketchpad. "Don't know. You said you had a story. Figured I'd see if it's any good."

A smirk tugged at Ray's lips. "Fair enough. But I'm not here to just talk at you. What's that?" He nodded toward the sketchpad, his tone casual but pointed.

Kai's fingers tightened around it, a flicker of wariness crossing his face. "Nothing. Just doodles."

"Doodles don't get held like that," Ray countered, his voice steady but gentle, coaxing rather than demanding. "Show me."

For a long moment, Kai didn't move, his jaw clenching as if debating whether to bolt. Ray waited, letting the silence stretch, knowing pressure would only push him away. Then, with a grunt of reluctant surrender, Kai flipped the pad open and shoved it across the table. Ray caught it before it slid off the edge, his breath catching as he took in the chaos spilled across the page.

It wasn't just a drawing—it was a storm captured in ink. Jagged lines spiralled into distorted faces, a cityscape warped into a nightmare of towering shadows and fractured streets. Hands—too many hands—clawed at the edges, reaching from a void that seemed to pulse with something alive, something desperate. The strokes were raw, unpolished, but they screamed with a fury Ray knew too well. This wasn't art for show; it was a confession, a map of a mind wrestling with a world it couldn't trust. It was the mental representation of what the world felt like to him.

"This isn't nothing," Ray said, his voice quiet but firm as he traced a finger along the twisted skyline. "This is you—right here. What it means?"

Kai shifted, his scowl deepening, but his eyes flicked up briefly, meeting Ray's before darting away. "It's what I see," he muttered, his voice low, almost lost in the room's hum. "The world's messed up. Everyone acts like it's fine—school, parents, all that crap—but it's not. Like there's something underneath, pulling strings, and no one gives a damn."

Ray's pulse quickened, a chill prickling his skin as Kai's words echoed Elias's warnings—*They watch. They enforce.* He leaned a little closer, keeping his tone even despite the jolt of recognition. "You're not wrong. There's more going on than most people see—or want to see. But you're looking. That's why you're here, isn't it?"

Kai's gaze snapped up again, holding Ray's this time, a spark of something—curiosity, maybe hope—breaking through the wall he'd built. "You saying you see it too?!"

"Yeah," Ray said, nodding toward the sketchpad. "I've seen it. Felt it. Two nights ago, I jumped off a rooftop— not to end it, but to prove something. That what we believe can change what's real. I landed because I knew I would."

Kai's brows shot up, scepticism warring with intrigue in his wide eyes. "That's insane."

"Maybe," Ray said, grinning despite the ache still lingering in his ribs from the fall. "But it worked. And this—" he tapped the sketchpad— "this is your jump. You're already seeing past the surface. Question is, what're you going to do with it?"

Kai stared at him, then down at the drawing, his fingers brushing the ink-stained edges as if testing their reality. "Don't know," he said, quieter now, thoughtful. "Keep drawing, I guess. Try to figure it out."

"Good," Ray said, leaning back. "Start there. Don't wait for someone to tell you it's okay. You've got something to say—say it. I'll help you, find the how."

Kai nodded slowly, a faint resolve tightening his posture, his scowl softening into something determined. Ray felt it then—the ripple beginning, a connection sparking to life. He'd leapt off that rooftop to prove his power to himself; now, he'd leap into this—mentoring Kai, guiding him toward the clarity Ray had fought to claim. It wasn't just about him anymore. It was about passing the fire, lighting a torch where he'd once let darkness reign.

The Test Returns

The centre's door slammed open, a sharp bang that shattered the fragile quiet. Ray's head snapped up, his body tensing as a familiar figure strode in—Zane Walker, broader and harder than the high school bully Ray remembered, his presence a dark stain against the room's muted chaos. His boots thudded against the linoleum, each step a deliberate challenge, his smirk sharp as a blade. The teens around them stilled, heads turning, a mix of unease and morbid fascination rippling through the air. Zane's eyes locked onto Ray, narrowing with a malice that hadn't dulled with time—not from high school, not from that alternate 2038 street where Ray had faced him down.

"Carter," Zane drawled, his voice slicing through the hum like a wire pulled taut. "Heard you're playing saviour now. Thought I'd check if the nobody's still got nothing to show."

Ray's stomach twisted, old reflexes surging—duck, shrink, let the words sink in like venom. Zane had always known how to find his weak spots, how to make him feel small, powerless. In 2042, he'd been a shadow Ray couldn't shake; in 2038, a test he'd passed by refusing to engage. But here, now, the stakes felt sharper—public, raw, with Kai and the others watching, their eyes wide and waiting. Ray exhaled, slow and deliberate, letting the fear flow through him like water over stone. Elias's lesson burned in his chest: *People only have power if you let them.* He'd beaten Zane before—twice—by choosing not to react. This was no different.

"Zane," Ray said, his voice flat, unshaken, as he rose from his chair. He squared his shoulders, keeping his hands loose at his sides, his posture open but steady. "What do you want?"

Zane stepped closer, his bulk filling the space, his shadow falling across the table. The room hushed, the teens leaning in, their whispers a soft undercurrent to the tension. Up close, Ray saw the cracks—bloodshot eyes, a faint tremor in his clenched fists, a desperation lurking beneath the bravado. Zane wasn't the giant Ray had built in his mind all those years ago; he was a man leaning on intimidation because it was all he had left.

"You think you're something now?" Zane sneered, his voice loud enough to carry, drawing every eye. "Talking big to these punks like you've got answers? You're still the same scared kid who'd run from me."

The jab stung, a barb aimed at the Ray who'd flinched, who'd believed he deserved it. A few teens shifted, murmurs rippling through the group—some doubtful, some curious. Kai watched, his sketchpad clutched tight, his gaze darting between them. Ray felt the weight of their stares, the pressure to prove himself, to react. His pulse quickened, adrenaline urging him to snap back, to show Zane he wasn't that kid anymore. But he didn't. He met Zane's glare with calm indifference, his voice steady. "You're loud, Zane. That's all you've got."

Zane's smirk faltered, a crack splitting his confidence. He lunged forward, shoving Ray's chest with both hands, the force rocking him back a step. Gasps echoed through the room, a girl in the corner flinching, a boy leaning forward as if expecting a brawl. Ray's ribs throbbed, the ache from the leap flaring, but he didn't waver. He straightened, his gaze locked on Zane's, letting the push slide off him like rain. "You done?" he asked, his tone flat, almost bored.

Zane's face twisted, confusion flashing through his narrowed eyes. He shoved again, harder, his knuckles digging into Ray's sternum. Pain spiked, sharp and hot, but Ray didn't flinch. He stood rooted, his hands still loose, watching as Zane's anger unravelled into bewilderment. The room shifted—murmurs turning to whispers of surprise, the tension souring into discomfort. A lanky kid with glasses muttered, "He's not even fighting back," and another turned away, losing interest in the one-sided clash.

"Fight me, damn it!" Zane snarled, grabbing Ray's jacket and yanking him forward, their faces inches apart. His breath reeked of stale beer, his eyes wild with a need Ray recognized—a need for control, for Ray to break and validate his power. Ray saw the tremble in his grip, the hollow edge to his rage. This wasn't strength; it was a man crumbling, begging for a reaction to prop him up.

"No," Ray said quietly, peeling Zane's hands off with slow, deliberate calm. He stepped back, his voice soft but firm. "I don't need to. You're just noise."

Zane staggered, thrown off by the refusal, his fists clenching and unclenching as his bravado shattered. The room watched, silent, as he muttered a curse, spat on the floor, and bolted for the door, slamming it behind him. The tension snapped, whispers erupting into a low buzz of awe. Kai's eyes widened, a grin tugging at his lips. "You didn't even blink," he said, half-statement, half-question.

Ray exhaled, adrenaline fading into a quiet thrill. "Didn't need to," he said, rubbing his chest where Zane's shove lingered. "He's only big if I let him be."

Kai nodded, the spark in his gaze flaring brighter—a spark Ray knew would grow. The others watched too, their slouched postures straightening, curiosity replacing apathy. Ray had passed the test—not just for himself, but for them. He'd shown them power wasn't in the fight; it was in the choice not to. And in that choice, he'd planted something—a seed of possibility in a room full of doubters.

Unveiling The Framework

Footsteps echoed from the hallway, slow and deliberate, cutting through the centre's renewed chatter. Ray turned, expecting a staff member to scold him for the disruption, but it was Elias—his silver hair glinting under the flickering fluorescents, his sharp eyes gleaming with a mix of approval and gravity. The room faded into a blur as he approached, his presence pulling Ray's focus like a strong magnet. The teens barely noticed, their attention drifting back to their phones, but Kai stayed alert, his sketchpad still clutched tight.

"You're getting good at that," Elias said, nodding toward the door Zane had stormed through. His voice was warm but edged with something deeper, a weight Ray couldn't yet place.

Ray rubbed his chest again, a faint grin breaking through. "Took everything not to swing. But it worked."

Elias crossed his arms, his smile fading into a graver line. "It's more than that, Ray. You're starting to see the framework—the unseen rules they've built to keep us predictable."

Ray's brow furrowed, the word *framework* sinking in like a stone. He leaned closer, lowering his voice. "You mean the enforcers?"

Elias nodded, his gaze darkening as he stepped nearer, his voice dropping to a near-whisper. "The ones who watch. The ones who tried to pull you back when you leapt. They're not just shadows—they're the architects. They've woven a system around us, a reality that thrives on reaction, on fear, on doubt. Every time you expect failure, every time you let someone like Zane dictate your state, you're feeding their design."

Ray's stomach tightened, the hum from the rooftop night flickering in his memory—a low pulse he'd felt but couldn't name. He glanced at Kai, then back to Elias. "So, what I did just now—standing there, letting it go—that's fighting them?"

"More than fighting," Elias said, his eyes piercing through the dim light. "It's breaking their hold. They can't control what doesn't react, *the one who makes his or her own choices*. You didn't just defy Zane—you defied the framework itself. And they don't like that."

Ray's mind raced, fragments of Elias's lessons snapping into place. The coffee cup changing from *Ryan* to *Ray*. The leap landing soft because he'd believed it would. The tests weren't random—they were cracks in a system he'd never seen, a system that wanted him small, reactive, predictable. "Why me?" he asked, his voice steady but urgent. "Why us?"

Elias's expression softened, a shadow of his own past flickering across his face. "Because I've seen what happens when you don't push back. Years ago, I let them win—let them shape my world into something I couldn't escape. I lost people to it—good people who didn't see the strings. A friend, once, who leapt like you did but didn't land. She believed their lies, and they erased her. When I found you, I saw a chance to undo that. You're not just a student, Ray—you're a crack in their machine."

The weight of it crashed over Ray, heavy but electrifying. He thought of Kai's drawings—the chaos beneath the surface, a kid's instinct mirroring what Elias described. "And Kai? The others?"

"They're part of it now," Elias said, glancing at the boy who watched with wide, unblinking eyes. "Every mind you wake up, every spark you light—it's a ripple they can't stop. But it's dangerous. The more you push, the harder they'll push back."

Ray clenched his fists, resolve hardening within him like steel forged in fire. "Let them try. I'm not stopping."

Elias's smile returned, faint but fierce, a glint of pride in his gaze. "Good. Because this framework—it's not unbreakable. It's just never been tested like this before. You are pushing it to its limits."

The room hummed faintly—an almost imperceptible vibration threading through the air, a sound Ray felt more than heard. Kai's head tilted, his voice low. "You hear that?"

"Yeah," Ray said, meeting Elias's gaze. "They're watching."

"Let them," Elias replied, his tone a quiet challenge. "They'll see what we're building."

Ray nodded, the fire in his chest flaring brighter. He'd leapt off a rooftop and landed whole. He'd faced Zane and walked away stronger. Now, he'd face this unseen framework—not just for himself, but for Kai, for Leila, for everyone who'd dare to see with him. The hum pulsed, a gauntlet thrown at his feet, but he didn't flinch. He turned to Kai, his voice steady. "Let's get to work. We've got a world to reshape."

Kai grinned, flipping his sketchpad to a fresh page, ink already staining his fingers. The teens around them stirred, drawn by the shift in the air—a shift Ray had sparked. The framework loomed, unseen but real, its architects watching from the shadows. But Ray wasn't afraid. He'd chosen his reality, *he had made his choice, and he'd keep choosing it*, every step, every spark, until the cracks became a chasm they couldn't close.

The centre buzzed with new energy, a canvas waiting for its first stroke. Ray squared his shoulders, he was ready for whatever came next.

Chapter - 12
The World Rewritten

> *"Reality is not a gift bestowed upon us—it is a garden we cultivate with every thought."*

> — **Anonymous**

The Seeds Of Change

Ray leaned against the cold metal railing of the community centre's rooftop, the city of 2042 stretching before him like a living mosaic of light and shadow. The night air carried the faint hum of drones and the distant pulse of thought-responsive billboards, their ads flickering in response to the minds below. His dark eyes traced the skyline, no longer seeing a prison of routine but a landscape ripe with possibility. His jacket, worn and patched from countless nights like this, flapped in the breeze—a relic of the Ray who'd once stood on rooftops contemplating nothingness, now a testament to the man he'd become.

The notebook Elias had given him rested in his pocket, its pages a growing chronicle of his journey—scribbled thoughts from leaps, lessons, and the quiet victories that had begun to ripple outward. Below, the community centre buzzed with life, its cracked windows spilling warm light onto the pavement. The mentorship program had taken root here, a handful of teens like Kai gathering weekly to wrestle with their own questions, their own realities. Ray had started it on a whim, a small step to test his newfound belief that perception could shape more than his own world. Now, it was something more—a seed planted in soil he'd once thought barren.

In a highly fertile ground, if you do nothing, weeds grow automatically, without any effort. However, if you want to make it a garden, then you have to make constant deliberate efforts to turn it into a garden. Even after it has become a beautiful garden, you have to constantly make efforts to make sure that the garden stays beautiful by weeding out the unwanted plantations and nurturing the wanted ones. *Our mind is just like a highly fertile ground.* If we do nothing about it, negative ideas come automatically, poisoning our mental state. If we have to have a positive mental state then we have to be constantly on the guard and weed out the unwanted negative doubts and ideas and deliberately choose and pursue the positive and empowering thoughts. Ray knew this fact inside out. He had experienced it.

He descended the stairs, the echo of his boots a steady rhythm against the concrete. The centre's main room greeted him with a cacophony of voices—teens arguing over a beat blaring from a cracked speaker, others hunched over sketchpads or laptops, their faces alight with focus. Kai stood at the centre, his wiry frame taut with energy as he showed off a new drawing—another chaotic cityscape, this one laced with streaks of vibrant colour cutting through the shadows. Ray paused in the doorway, watching the boy's hands move with a confidence he hadn't seen a month ago.

"Ray!" Kai called, spotting him. His dark eyes gleamed with a mix of pride and challenge as he waved the sketchpad. "Check this out—better than last time, right?"

Ray crossed the room, taking the pad with a nod. The drawing was raw, unpolished, but alive—streets twisted into spirals, faces emerging from the chaos, and those streaks of colour slicing through like hope breaking dawn. "It's more than better," Ray said, handing it back. "It's you—really you. What's the story here?"

Kai shrugged, but a grin tugged at his lips. "It's the city, but not how they want us to see it. It's messy, yeah, but there's something in it—something worth fighting for."

Ray's chest tightened, a quiet thrill sparking within him. Kai's words echoed his own journey—seeing beyond the surface, finding meaning in the mess. "Keep going," he said, clapping the boy on the shoulder. "You're onto something."

The others glanced up, their chatter softening as Ray moved among them. A girl with purple streaks in her hair—Lena—held up a poem scribbled on a napkin, her voice trembling but fierce as she read it aloud. A lanky boy named Tariq tapped at a laptop, coding a game inspired by Ray's stories of shifting realities. Each one was a spark, a thread in a tapestry Ray hadn't planned but couldn't deny. He'd leapt off a rooftop to prove his belief could bend the world; now, he was helping them leap too—not with their bodies, but with their minds.

Later, as the group dispersed into the night, Ray lingered at the table, flipping open his notebook. He'd started writing again—not just notes, but something bigger. A book, raw and unfiltered, weaving his experiences into a call to wake up, *to choose*, to create. The words flowed easier now, each sentence a brick in a foundation he hadn't known he could build. He'd sent the first chapters to a friend who knew a publisher, half-expecting rejection. Instead, he'd gotten a reply: *This could change things. Keep going.* The thought sent a shiver through him—not of doubt, but of possibility.

The Blade Of Betrayal

The door creaked open, pulling Ray from his thoughts. Kai slipped back inside, his sketchpad tucked under his arm, his usual swagger replaced by a tension Ray couldn't place. The boy hesitated, his sneakers scuffing the floor, then tossed a folded paper onto the table. "You need to see this," he said, his voice low, edged with something sharp—guilt, maybe, or defiance.

Ray unfolded it, his eyes scanning the text. His breath caught as the words sank in—a letter, typed and unsigned, but its intent was clear: *Ray Carter's mentorship is a delusion. He's feeding you lies about controlling your life. Stop listening, or we'll stop him.* Beneath it, scrawled in Kai's jagged handwriting: *I gave this to them. I'm sorry.*

The room tilted, a cold wave crashing over Ray. He looked up, meeting Kai's gaze—eyes darting, shoulders hunched, waiting for the blow. "Them?" Ray asked, his voice steady despite the storm brewing inside. "Who's 'them'?"

Kai swallowed, his hands balling into fists. "Guys I used to run with—older kids, tough ones. They don't like what you're doing here. Said you're messing with people's heads, making us think we're something we're not. They offered me cash to... to shut it down."

Ray's fingers tightened around the paper. He had experienced betrayal before, but this time the sting of betrayal was cutting deeper than he'd expected. Kai had been his first spark, the kid he'd seen himself in—the lost boy searching for a way out. He'd trusted him, poured hours into guiding him, and now this—a knife in the back, handed to shadows who wanted Ray silenced. The old him would've reacted—yelled, accused, let the hurt define the moment. Anger flared, hot and bitter, urging him to lash out.

But he didn't. He exhaled, slow and deliberate, letting the emotion pass through him like smoke. Elias's voice echoed in his skull: *You control your reaction. That's your power.* This wasn't just a betrayal—it was a test, another crucible to prove what he'd learned. Kai wasn't the enemy; he was a kid caught in a web Ray hadn't seen coming.

"Why?" Ray asked, his tone calm but piercing, holding Kai's gaze.

Kai's defiance cracked, his voice trembling and breaking. "I didn't mean it—not at first. They got in my head, said you're some freak, that this—" he gestured to the room— "is all fake. I needed the money, Ray. My mom's sick, and I… I messed up." Tears started to roll out in a flurry on his dry cheeks.

The confession hung between them, raw and heavy. Ray saw it then—the tremble in Kai's hands, the shame in his eyes, the weight of a choice he hadn't known how to escape. It didn't erase the hurt, but it shifted it, reframed it. This wasn't about Ray—it was about Kai's fear, his doubt, the same shadows Ray had once let rule him.

"You could've told me," Ray said, folding the letter and setting it aside. "We could've figured it out together."

Kai's head dropped, his voice barely a whisper. "I thought you'd hate me."

"Hate's a choice," Ray said, standing. "And I'm not choosing it. You screwed up, yeah. But you came back, *you made a choice*. That counts."

Kai blinked, confusion warring with relief. "You're not kicking me out?"

"No, never," Ray said, stepping closer. "But you're going to fix this. You know who they are—tell me. We'll deal with it together."

Kai nodded, a spark reigniting in his eyes—a spark Ray wouldn't let die. The betrayal stung, but it didn't own him. He'd rewrite this moment, not with anger, but with trust he will rebuilt it, *he made his choice*. The shadows Kai had handed that letter to—they weren't just street toughs. Ray felt it, a hum threading through the air, the same vibration he'd sensed with the enforcers. This was bigger, a ripple from the framework Elias had warned him about.

The Cost Of Defiance

The rooftop beckoned again, its silence a stark contrast to the centre's chaos. Ray climbed the stairs, Kai's confession still echoing in his mind, and found Elias waiting near the edge, his silver hair catching the city's glow. The older man's presence was a quiet storm, his eyes sharp with a mix of pride and unease.

"You're stirring things up," Elias said, his voice low but resonant. "The mentorship, the writing—it's spreading."

Ray leaned against the railing, the letter crumpled in his pocket. "Kai sold me out. Gave some group a heads-up to shut me down. Said they're scared of what I'm doing."

Elias's gaze darkened, his posture stiffening. "Not just a group. The enforcers—or their proxies. They don't move directly unless they have to. They use others—the pawns who don't even know they're being played."

Ray's stomach tightened, the hum pulsing faintly at the edge of his senses. "They're coming for me, aren't they?"

"They're already here," Elias said, stepping closer. "You're rewriting the world, Ray—not just yours, but theirs too. Every kid you wake up, every word you write, it's a crack in their framework. They'll push back harder now. Betrayal's just the start. It's not the end. They have many more methods to break you, that is, if you allow them to."

Ray's fists clenched, the weight of it sinking in. He'd leapt off rooftops, faced Zane, forgiven Leila's betrayal— but this was different. This wasn't just about him. This was a war, not just against his own doubts, but against something vast and unseen which effects everyone. "What happens if I keep going?" he asked, his voice steady despite the storm inside. "What's the cost?"

Elias's eyes softened, a rare vulnerability breaking through. "Everything. Your safety, your peace—maybe more. I lost someone once—a girl who saw too much, pushed too far. They erased her, Ray. Not killed—erased. Like she never was. I couldn't stop it."

The confession hit Ray like a punch, a glimpse into Elias's scars, his stakes. "And you think that'll happen to me?"

"I think it could," Elias said, his tone grave. "But you're different. You're not just seeing—you're building. That book, those kids—it's a shield they didn't expect. The more you spread this, the harder it is to erase you. But it'll cost you."

Ray exhaled, the city's hum vibrating through him—a challenge, a threat, a call. He thought of Kai's drawings, Lena's poems, Tariq's code—the sparks he'd lit, the lives he'd touched. He thought of the manuscript growing on his desk, the words that could wake a world. The cost was immense and real, but so was the gain. "I'm not stopping," he said, meeting Elias's gaze. "If they want me, they'll have to fight every single one of us."

He had not only made his choice, he was also willing to pay the price of his choice.

Elias's smile was faint but fierce. "Then you're ready for what's coming."

The hum sharpened, shadows shifting along the rooftop's edge—an echo of the enforcers' reach. Ray squared his shoulders, the fire in his chest blazing brighter. He'd rewritten his reality, faced betrayal, and chosen to stand. The world below wasn't just his anymore—it was theirs, a garden he'd cultivate with every thought, every act of defiance.

"Let them come," he said, his voice a quiet thunder. "I'll rewrite them too."

The city stretched before him, alive with possibilities. Ray gripped the railing, ready for the fight—for the cost, for the creation. The framework could watch, could threaten, but it couldn't stop what he'd begun. Not now. Not ever.

Chapter - 13
The Enforcers Emerge

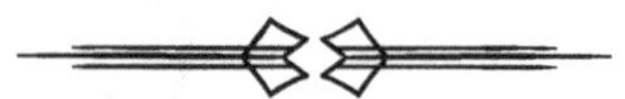

"The greatest battles are fought not with the weapons, but with the will to stand unbowed."

— **Anonymous**

The Stirring Shadows

Ray sat at the cluttered desk in his apartment, the dim glow of a flickering desk lamp casting jagged shadows across the room. The city of 2042 hummed beyond his window, its artificial lights painting the night sky in shades of amber and steel. His journal lay open before him, ink-stained pages chronicling his leaps—literal and figurative—since that first shift through the rooftop door. The key Elias had given him rested beside it, a quiet weight that anchored him to the reality he'd reclaimed. His fingers traced its edges, worn smooth from restless nights like this, as his mind churned with a question he couldn't shake: *What comes next?*

The mentorship at the community centre had taken firm root, its tendrils were fast spreading through Kai and the others, their voices growing louder, their creations bolder. His book—scribbled drafts now coalescing into something tangible—had begun to ripple outward, a friend promising to pass it to a publisher who saw its spark. Ray felt the shift, a tide turning within him and beyond him, but with it came a tremor—an unease threading through the air, a hum he couldn't ignore. It wasn't the city's usual pulse; it was something sharper, something watching.

He stood, stretching his aching limbs, and paced to the window. The street below buzzed with late-night life— hover-cars gliding silently, pedestrians hunched against the chill—but something felt off. A streetlamp flickered, its rhythm erratic, not in sync with the others. A shadow stretched unusually too long across the pavement, unmoving despite the wind tugging at everything else. Ray's breath fogged the glass as he leaned closer, his pulse quickening. He could hear his own heartbeat. The hum grew louder, a vibration seeping through the walls, threading into his bones like a warning he couldn't decipher.

He turned, scanning the room, and froze. His phone, resting on the desk, flickered—its screen glitching with static before displaying a message he hadn't typed: *You've gone too far.* The words pulsed once, then vanished, leaving the screen dark again. Ray's stomach twisted, a cold dread prickling his skin. He grabbed the device, his thumb hovering over Leila's contact, but hesitated. Elias's voice echoed in his skull: *They watch. They enforce.* Was this them—the enforcers he'd been warned about, the shadows lurking at the edges of his reality?

The lamp flickered again, plunging the room into brief darkness. When the light returned, a note sat on his journal—folded, pristine, as if placed by an unseen hand. Ray's hands trembled as he opened it, the words scrawled in sharp, precise letters: *Turn back, or we will erase you.* His throat tightened, the air thickening with a presence he couldn't see but felt, pressing against his chest like a silent threat. The hum sharpened, a low roar that rattled the windowpane, and for a moment, the shadows outside slowly twisted—forming shapes too deliberate to be the tricks of light.

Ray stepped back, his mind racing. This wasn't paranoia; this was real. The enforcers weren't just a warning—they were here, their reach seeping into his world, testing the edges of his resolve. He'd rewritten reality before—coffee cups, leaps, confrontations—but this was different. This was a storm gathering, and he was at its centre.

Leila's Fracture

The café door chimed as Ray pushed through it the next morning, the familiar scent of roasted beans and old books wrapping around him like a lifeline. Leila sat at their usual table, her curly hair spilling over her shoulders, her fingers tapping restlessly against a chipped mug. She looked up as he approached, her sharp brown eyes narrowing with a mix of relief and something darker—something guarded.

"You're late," she said, her tone lighter than her expression suggested. "Thought you'd finally bailed on me."

Ray slid into the chair across from her, forcing a smirk despite the weight pressing against his ribs. "Takes more than an existential crisis to keep me away."

She didn't laugh—not the sharp, bright sound he'd come to rely on. Instead, she leaned back, crossing her arms, her gaze darting to the window before settling on him. "You've been off lately," she said, her voice low, probing. "What's going on, Ray?"

He hesitated, the note burning a hole in his pocket, its warning a splinter in his mind. He wanted to tell her—about the hum, the shadows, the message—but something held him back. She'd been his anchor, the one who'd always pulled him from the ledge, but the air between them felt brittle, fragile in a way it hadn't before, never.

"Leila," he started, leaning forward, "have you noticed anything… strange? Lights flickering, messages that shouldn't be there?"

Her eyes widened, a flicker of recognition crossing her face before she masked it with a frown. "What are you talking about?"

Ray's stomach sank. She was hiding something—he could feel it, a crack in the trust they'd built. He reached into his pocket, pulling out the note and sliding it across the table. "This showed up last night. No one was there. It just… appeared."

Leila unfolded it, her fingers trembling slightly as she read the words. Her jaw tightened, her breath hitching, and when she looked up, guilt shadowed her eyes. "Ray, I…" She stopped, swallowing hard. "I need to tell you something."

The café faded, the hum of conversation dimming as dread coiled in his chest. "What?"

She pushed a folded paper toward him—a letter, its edges worn, her handwriting unmistakable. Ray's hands shook as he opened it, scanning the text. It was addressed to someone unnamed, detailing his mentorship, his book, his leaps—everything he'd shared with her in confidence. At the bottom, a single line: *He's becoming a threat. Stop him.*

Ray's vision blurred, the words searing into him like a brand. He looked up, meeting her gaze, and saw the tears welling in her eyes. "You wrote this," he said with disbelief, his voice raw and shaky, barely above a whisper. "You gave them!"

"I didn't mean to," she said, her voice breaking. "They came to me—weeks ago. Said they'd hurt you if I didn't help. I thought… I thought I could protect you by keeping them close, feeding them just enough to keep them off your back. But I was wrong, Ray. I'm so sorry." Her guilt laden voice was shaking.

The betrayal cut deeper than Kai's had, sharper than any test he'd faced. Leila wasn't just a friend—she was his tether, the one who'd believed in him when he couldn't. And now, she'd handed his dreams to the shadows threatening to erase him. Anger surged, hot and jagged, urging him to lash out, to sever the bond that had held him together. But he stopped, inhaling slowly, letting Elias's lesson anchor him: *You control your reaction.*

"Why didn't you tell me?" he asked, now his voice was steady despite the storm within.

"I was scared, scared for you" she whispered, tears spilling over. "Scared they'd take you away—like they took Evan. You are all that I have in life. I couldn't lose you too."

Evan. Her brother, lost to despair she couldn't pull him from. The pieces clicked, her guilt and fear laid bare. Ray's chest ached, the anger fading into something softer, more complex. She'd betrayed him, yes, but not out of malice—out of a desperate need to save him, twisted by the enforcers' leverage. It is not always about the result of the action; the intention behind the action matters the most. *Ray made the choice of focusing on her intention rather than the result of her action.*

"You should've trusted me," he said, folding the letter and sliding it back. "We could've faced them together."

"I know," she said, her voice trembling. "I messed up. I'll do anything to fix it."

Ray studied her, the fire of betrayal cooling into rock solid resolve. This wasn't the end of their bond—it was a fracture he could mend, a test he could rewrite. "Then help me fight them," he said. "No more secrets."

She nodded, wiping her eyes, a spark of her old fierceness returning. "No more secrets." It was not a promise, it was a resolve.

Elias's Truth

The rooftop loomed under a bruised sky, its rusted door a silent sentinel as Ray climbed the stairs, Leila at his side. The hum pulsed stronger now, a low roar threading through the air, shadows shifting along the edges of his vision. Elias waited near the railing, his silver hair catching the faint light, his sharp eyes glinting with urgency as they approached.

"You felt them," Elias said, his voice cutting through the wind. "They're here."

Ray nodded, handing him the note. "They left this. And Leila—" He glanced at her, her jaw tight with shame. "They got to her too."

Elias unfolded the paper, his expression darkening as he read. "They're moving faster than I thought," he muttered, crumpling it in his fist. "You've pushed too far, Ray. They're not just watching anymore—they're acting."

"Who are they?" Ray demanded, stepping closer. "You keep hinting, warning me, but what are they?"

Elias exhaled, his gaze drifting to the horizon, shadowed with a past he rarely spoke of. "They're the enforcers of the framework—the architects of this reality's boundaries. They're not human—not anymore. Once, they were like us, seekers who saw beyond the veil. But they chose control over freedom, power over choice. They built a system to keep the world predictable, to stop anyone from bending it like you have."

Ray's stomach tightened, the hum vibrating through him like a heartbeat. "And you know this because…?"

"Because I fought them," Elias said, his voice low, heavy with memory. "Years ago, I leapt like you did—saw the edges of their design. I had a partner, Mara—she was fearless, brilliant. We pushed too hard, tried to break their hold. They erased her, Ray. Not killed—erased. I woke up one day, and she was gone—no trace, no memory in anyone but me. I've been running ever since, guiding others to finish what we started."

The confession hung between them, a wound laid bare. Ray's chest ached, the stakes sharpening into focus. "And now they want me gone too."

"Yes," Elias said, meeting his gaze. "Your book, your mentorship—it's waking people up, cracking their framework. They'll do anything to stop that."

Ray clenched his fists, the fire in his chest flaring brighter and hotter. "Then why didn't they erase me already?"

Elias's smile was faint but fierce. "Because you're stronger than they expected. You don't just see—you act. Every leap, every choice—it's a rebellion they can't predict. But they'll try harder now."

Leila stepped forward, her voice steady despite her earlier tears. "So, what do we do?"

Elias looked between them, his eyes glinting with resolve. "You fight—not with fists, but with belief. They thrive on reaction, on fear, on doubt, on self-disbelief. Deny them that, and you weaken them."

Ray nodded, the hum a challenge he'd meet head-on. "Then we keep pushing—me, Leila, Kai, everyone. If they want me, they'll have to take us all." Leila nodded affirmatively.

Elias's smile widened, a spark of pride cutting through the darkness. "That's the spirit. But be ready—their next move will test you like nothing before."

The shadows shifted, the hum rising to a low roar. Ray squared his shoulders, Leila at his side, Elias's truth a torch lighting the way. The enforcers had emerged, their threat no longer a whisper but a storm. But Ray wasn't alone, and he wasn't afraid. He'd rewrite this battle, not just for himself, but for the world he'd begun to reshape.

Nothing and no one can stop a person who has found a meaning, a purpose in life which transcends self and encapsulates the humanity. Ray wasn't doing the things for himself, he wanted to liberate the entire humanity.

"Let them come," he said, his voice a quiet thunder. "I'll show them what I'm made of."

Ray wasn't just telling it, he had already decided that. Though he didn't know how exactly how he was going to do it but he knew he will find a way. *He had made his choice irrespective of the outcome of his efforts.*

The rooftop stretched silent around them, the city alive below—a canvas waiting for its next stroke.

Chapter - 14
The Mirror Within

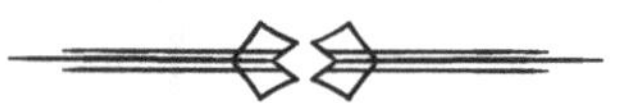

"We do not see the things as they are;
we see them as we are."

— **Anaïs Nin**

Reflections Of The Past

Ray stood in the dimly lit alley, the city's hum a distant murmur against the stillness that followed his latest shift. The air was cool, clinging to his skin like a second shadow, and his breath curled into the night in faint wisps. His boots scuffed the cracked pavement, echoing softly as he paced, his mind still reeling from the enforcers' emergence—their distorted forms, their chilling threat of erasure. He'd faced them with Leila and Elias on the rooftop, *chosen defiance over surrender irrespective of the outcome*, and returned to 2042 intact. But the victory felt fragile, a thin veneer over a growing unease that gnawed at his core.

The streetlamp above flickered, casting erratic pools of light that danced across the walls. Ray paused, his gaze snagging on his reflection in a puddle—dark hair tousled, eyes shadowed with exhaustion, jacket patched from too many falls. He looked like himself, but something about the image unsettled him. It rippled, not with the wind, but with a tremor that seemed to come from within. His breath hitched as the reflection shifted, the face morphing into a younger version of himself—sixteen, hollow-cheeked, staring back with the dull glaze of a boy who'd already given up.

Ray stumbled back, his heart thudding against his ribs. The puddle stilled, but the alley around him shimmered, walls bending like liquid glass. Shadows stretched and twisted, forming figures—no, not figures, but echoes of him. To his left stood the Ray from that rooftop two years ago, hands gripping the ledge, eyes fixed on the abyss below. To his right, another—eighteen, slouched in his bedroom, college application was open on a screen that he'd never submit. Each reflection wore his face but carried a different weight, a different story etched into their postures, their gazes.

"What the hell is this?" Ray muttered, his voice trembling as he spun to face them. The echoes didn't move, didn't speak, but their presence pressed against him—a gallery of past failures, regrets he'd buried under layers of newfound resolve. The sixteen-year-old's eyes accused him: *You let me waste away.* The eighteen-year-old's sneer mocked him: *You never had the guts.* Ray's fists clenched, his nails digging into his palms as he fought the urge to look away. These weren't just memories—they were alive, tangible, a mirror he couldn't shatter.

The air pulsed, the hum sharpening into a low roar. The reflections stepped closer, their silent judgment tightening around him like a noose. Ray's chest heaved, panic clawing at his throat. He'd rewritten reality—coffee cups, leaps, confrontations with Zane—but this was different. These were pieces of himself he'd left behind, fragments he'd thought he'd escaped. Had the enforcers done this? Were they twisting his mind, forcing him to face what he'd refused to see?

Footsteps broke the silence—a familiar rhythm cutting through the haze. Leila emerged from the alley's mouth, her curly hair catching the flickering light, her sharp brown eyes narrowing as she took in the scene. "Ray?" she called, her voice steady but laced with concern. "What's going on?"

He turned to her, relief warring with dread. "You see them too?"

She nodded slowly, stepping closer, her gaze darting between the reflections. "Yeah. But they're not…" Her words faltered as a shadow rose beside her—a younger Leila, maybe fifteen, her face pale and tear-streaked, clutching a worn photo Ray couldn't make out. Leila froze, her breath catching, and for the first time since he'd known her, she looked small, vulnerable.

"Evan," she whispered, her voice breaking on the name. Ray's stomach twisted—he knew that name, the brother she'd lost, the wound she'd buried beneath her relentless drive. The younger Leila stared back, her eyes hollow with a grief Ray could feel, a mirror of the pain she'd carried into every push, every insistence that he keep going.

Ray understood what the enforcers were trying to do. They were trying to rip open the old wounds which were healed. They were trying to break their resolve. They were trying to make them to go back to their old selves where they were not in control of their destiny. They were trying to revive their old conditioning out of which they had come out.

Leila's Mirror

Ray reached for her, his hand brushing her arm, grounding her as she'd grounded him so many times before. "Leila, look at me," he said, his voice firm despite the chaos around them. "They're not real, they are not us—not the way we are now."

She tore her gaze from the reflection, her eyes glistening but fierce. "Then why are they here?" she snapped, her tone sharp with a mix of anger and fear. "Why is he here?"

Ray tightened his grip, steadying them both. "I don't know. But I think… I think this is about us—about what we've been running away from." He glanced at his own echoes, their silent accusations ringing louder in his skull. "They're us, Leila. The parts of us that we didn't face."

Leila's jaw tightened, her breath shuddering as she turned back to the younger her. "I couldn't save him," she said, her voice raw, trembling with a confession she'd never spoken aloud. "Evan was drowning—drugs, despair, everything—and I tried, Ray. I tried so hard, but he slipped away. I found him cold on the bathroom floor, and I couldn't…" She stopped, choking on the words, tears spilling over despite her clenched fists.

Ray's chest ached, not just for her pain but for the echo it stirred in him—the nights he'd lain awake, convinced he'd never be enough, letting opportunities slip because he'd expected failure. "You didn't fail him," he said, his voice low but certain. "You were a kid too. You did what you could. You gave your best, even if after giving your best couldn't save him, it's not your fault Leila."

She shook her head, her gaze locked on the reflection. "I should've done more. I should've seen it. That's why I push you—why I can't let you give up. I can't lose someone else."

The younger Leila stepped closer, her hollow eyes softening—not with forgiveness, but with something like understanding. Ray saw it then—the weight Leila carried wasn't just guilt; it was a vow, a promise she made to herself to never let another spark fade. He turned to his own reflections, the sixteen-year-old's despair, the eighteen-year-old's apathy. They weren't here to punish him—they were here to show him what he'd overcome, what he could still become.

"I see you," he said to them, his voice steadying as he faced each one. "I was you—scared, lost, waiting for something to change. But I'm not you anymore. *I don't wait for things to happen, not anymore. I make things happen. I chose different.*"

The reflections wavered, their edges blurring as if his words had loosened their hold. Leila took a shaky breath, stepping toward her younger self. "I'm sorry," she said, her voice breaking but resolute. "I couldn't save you, Evan. But I'm still here, and I'm fighting—for me, for Ray, for everyone I can reach."

The younger Leila's form flickered, a faint smile ghosting across her lips before she dissolved into shadow. Ray's echoes followed, the sixteen-year-old's gaze lifting with a flicker of hope, the eighteen-year-old's sneer fading into quiet acceptance. The alley steadied, the hum softening to a whisper, the walls snapping back into solidity.

Elias's Revelation

Footsteps echoed again, slower this time, deliberate. Elias emerged from the shadows, his silver hair glinting under the streetlamp, his sharp eyes scanning the now-empty space where the reflections had stood. "You faced them," he said, his voice warm with approval but edged with something heavier—something weary.

Ray turned to him, Leila at his side, her arm brushing his in silent solidarity. "What were they?" he asked, his voice hoarse but firm. "The enforcers?"

Elias shook his head, stepping closer. "Not directly. They're echoes—mirrors of your own making, pulled from your mind by the framework. The enforcers don't create them; they amplify them, use them to break you from within."

Ray's brow furrowed, the pieces clicking into place. "So, they're us—our doubts, our fears, our insecurities, our feeling of inadequacy?"

"Exactly," Elias said, crossing his arms. "The enforcers aren't the Gods—they're the parasites. They were human once, seekers like us who glimpsed the truth: that perception shapes reality. But instead of freeing it, they bound it. They built a system—a framework—to trap humanity into predictable loops, feeding on our reactions, our surrender. When we doubt, when we fear, we give them power. These mirrors? They're their tools, reflections of what holds us back."

Leila wiped her eyes, her voice steadying. "Evan—he wasn't real. Just a shadow they pulled out of me."

Elias nodded, his gaze softening. "A shadow you faced. That's why it faded. The enforcers thrive on what we refuse to see. When you decide to confront it, you strip their leverage. Face what you fear the most and its death is certain."

Ray's mind raced, Elias's words weaving into everything he'd learned. The coffee cup changing from *Ryan* to *Ray*. The leap that landed soft because he'd believed it would. The tests weren't just about bending reality—they were about bending himself, facing the parts he'd buried. "So, they're using our own minds against us, it's about setting our mind against us!" he said, his voice low but resolute. "But if I control my mind, *if I control what I choose to see…*"

"*Then you control what they can do,*" Elias finished, a faint smile tugging at his lips.

"They're not invincible, Ray. They're shadows cast by human belief—ours, and everyone else's. The more you see, the less they can hide. It's a secret that is hiding in plain sight, yet everyone doesn't get to see it. People choose what they want to see, you chose differently."

Ray exhaled, the weight of it settling over him—not as a burden, but as a challenge. He thought of the hum, the flickering shadows, the enforcers' threats. They weren't just after him—they were after the movement he'd sparked, the awakening he'd begun, the awareness he was spreading. But they'd miscalculated. Every mirror he faced, every fear he conquered, made him stronger, not weaker.

"Why show us this now?" Leila asked, her voice sharp with lingering pain. "Why not before?"

Elias's expression darkened, a shadow of his own past flickering across his face. "Because they're desperate now. Initially they thought you are just a glitch which will fade away like the most of people. But, you're not just a glitch anymore—you're a threat to their existence. I've seen them destroy others—people like Mara, who pushed too far without knowing the cost. I couldn't save her. But you…" He met Ray's gaze, then Leila's. "You're ready to fight back."

Ray clenched his fists, the fire in his chest blazing brighter. "Then we will do it. Together."

Leila nodded, her resolve mirroring his own. "No more running. No more shadows."

Elias's smile returned, fierce and unyielding. "Good. Because the mirrors are just the beginning. They'll come at you harder now—twist what you love, what you fear. But you've got the tools. Use them."

The alley stretched silent around them, the city's hum a quiet backdrop to their stand. Ray looked at Leila, her strength a tether he'd never lose, then at Elias, his wisdom a torch lighting the way. The reflections were gone, but their lessons remained—etched into his mind, his choices, his reality. The enforcers could watch, could threaten, but they couldn't stop him *till he is in control of his choices. Not now, when he was willing to pay the price of his choices and, he did not want anything for himself, he had set himself the goal of liberating the world.* Problems are those fearful things that you see when you take your eyes off your goal. When you want to jump you focus on the place where you want to jump to, you don't focus your eyes on your feet. Likewise, when your goal is clear then all you see is the goal, whatever problems you encounter on the way are incidental, they not your focus.

"Let's go," Ray said, stepping forward, his voice a quiet thunder. "We've got a world to rewrite."

The night unfolded before them, alive with possibilities—a canvas they'd claimed, together.

Chapter - 15
The Cost Of Seeing

"To see the truth is to bear its weight—ignorance is a luxury you can no longer afford."

— Anonymous

The Weight Of Doubt

Ray stood at the front of the community centre's meeting room, the air heavy with the scent of damp concrete and the faint tang of spilled energy drinks. The fluorescent lights flickered overhead, casting a harsh, uneven glow across the chipped wooden table and the mismatched chairs where his mentees sat. Their faces—once alight with curiosity and defiance—were now shadowed with uncertainty, their voices a low murmur of questions Ray wasn't sure he could answer. His journal rested open before him, its ink-stained pages a testament to the battles he'd fought: the leap from the rooftop, the sterile prison of the enforcers, the moment he'd bent reality to escape their grasp. His hands bore faint scrapes from that fall, a quiet reminder of his survival, but tonight, as he faced these kids, that victory felt fragile, a thin thread stretched taut over a growing abyss.

The room had been his sanctuary—a haven where he'd watched Kai's sketches evolve from jagged chaos to bold visions, where Lena's poems had cut through silence like a blade, where Tariq's code had woven possibilities into something tangible. They'd been a circle of trust, a spark he'd nurtured with his own journey from apathy to agency. He'd shared his story—not the polished version, but the raw one: the nights he'd stood on rooftops contemplating nothingness, the shifts through alternate realities, the power he'd found in choosing his response. They'd listened, wide-eyed, and begun to see their own potential, their own power to shape their worlds. But now, that trust wavered, fractured by a shadow Ray hadn't anticipated.

Kai slouched in his chair near the back, his dark hair falling over his eyes, his arms crossed tight across his chest. His sketchpad lay unopened on the table, its edges worn from constant use, but tonight, it stayed shut—a silent rebuke. Beside him, Lena gripped a crumpled napkin, her latest poem scrawled in shaky ink, her purple-streaked hair veiling her face as she avoided Ray's gaze. Tariq sat stiffly, his laptop dark, his usual restless tapping replaced by a stillness that felt like a wall. The newer faces—teens drawn by whispers of Ray's book and talks—shifted uneasily, their murmurs a low buzz of doubt that stung more than Ray wanted to admit.

He cleared his throat, his voice cutting through the tension like a dull blade. "Okay, let's get started. What's on your minds tonight?"

Kai's head snapped up, his scowl sharp and unyielding. "What's the point, Ray? You keep saying we can change things—make our lives mean something—but what if it's all a lie?"

The words landed like a blow, heavier than Zane's shoves, deeper than Leila's betrayal. Ray's chest tightened, his breath catching as he met Kai's gaze. This wasn't just skepticism—it was a fracture in the foundation he'd built, a crack the enforcers had widened with their subtle, insidious interference. Kai had been his first mentee, the kid who'd mirrored his own lost years, the one who'd begun to believe in the power of perception. Now, that belief was crumbling, and Ray felt it like a personal failure.

"What do you mean?" he asked, keeping his tone even, though his pulse hammered in his ears.

Kai shoved a crumpled flyer across the table, its edges torn as if ripped from a wall in anger. Ray caught it, smoothing it out with unsteady hands, his stomach sinking as he read the bold, accusatory text: *Ray Carter's Lies: Don't Trust the Dreamer. He'll Lead You to Nothing.* Beneath it, a grainy photo of him speaking at the centre, his face circled in red ink—a target. The words echoed the enforcers' warnings—*You've gone too far, turn back*—but this wasn't their pristine script. This was human, messy, a ripple of their influence spreading through the streets, turning his own words against him.

"Where'd this come from?" Ray asked, his voice low but firm, his eyes flicking back to Kai.

"Everywhere," Kai snapped, his fists clenching on the table. "Streets, school, my mom's shop—someone's plastering them all over town. People are saying you're full of it, Ray—that all this—" he gestured to the room, the sketchpads, the laptops— "is just some fantasy you cooked up to feel important. And after last week, with those weird glitches, I'm starting to think they're right."

Ray's mind flashed to the disturbances—the flickering streetlights outside his apartment, the static on his phone screen, the whispers in empty rooms that had trailed him since his escape from the enforcers' prison. Subtle, calculated moves to sow doubt, to undermine the trust he'd built. He'd felt the hum threading through the city, a vibration he'd dismissed as aftershocks of his leap, but now he saw it for what it was: their hand, reaching into his world, striking at its roots.

Lena's voice broke through, soft but edged with defiance. "My brother saw it too," she said, her fingers tightening around her napkin until the ink smeared. "He said you're dragging us into something dangerous—that we're going to get hurt following you. What if he's right, Ray? What if this costs us more than we can handle?"

The room erupted into a low rumble, voices overlapping—some agreeing with Lena's fear, others defending Ray with hesitant conviction, all laced with a raw unease that twisted in his gut. He'd faced the enforcers' sterile threats, their promise of erasure, but this—this doubt in the eyes of the kids he'd sworn to guide—cut deeper than any blade they could wield. His hands pressed against the table, grounding him as the weight of their uncertainty threatened to pull him under.

He raised a hand, the gesture sharp enough to silence them. "Listen," he said, his voice steady despite the storm raging within him. "I get it. You're scared—things are getting weird, and now these flyers are everywhere, messing with your heads. But let me ask you something: did you feel it when you started here? That moment when you realized you could be more than what everyone expects?"

Kai's scowl softened, a flicker of memory breaking through his defences—the nights he'd stayed late sketching, the pride in his voice when he'd shared his first bold piece. Lena nodded reluctantly, her grip loosening on the napkin as she recalled the tremor in her voice giving way to strength when she'd read her poem aloud. Tariq glanced up, his fingers twitching as if itching to type, remembering the rush of coding a world where he controlled the rules. Ray seized that spark, his words urgent but firm.

"That wasn't a lie," he pressed, leaning forward. "It's real—it's yours. I'm not spinning some fairy tale to trick you. I've lived it—leapt off rooftops, faced people who wanted me gone, and came out the other side because I believed I could, *I chose to believe*. But yeah, *it comes with a cost*. Seeing the truth always does—it's messy, it's scary, and sometimes it means standing alone. You've got a choice now: walk away, let the doubt win, go back to your former selves pretending none of this matters. Or stay, and fight for what you've started to see. It's your life, *you make the choice*."

The silence that followed was thick, heavy with the weight of decision. Ray's breath steadied, his gaze sweeping the room, meeting each pair of eyes—some wavering, some hardening with resolve. He felt the hum again, faint but persistent, a whisper beneath the floorboards, a reminder of the enforcers' reach. They hadn't just come for him—they'd aimed at this circle, at the trust he'd forged with these kids. But he wouldn't let it break—not without giving them the chance to *choose for themselves*.

Kai's jaw worked, his eyes darting to the flyer, then back to Ray. "What if they're right, though?" he asked, his voice quieter now, less defiant. "What if this blows up in our faces?"

Ray leaned closer, his tone dropping to a fierce whisper that carried across the room. "Then we face it together. I've been where you are—doubting everything, scared it's easier to give up. But I didn't, and I'm still here. *You decide* what's worth it, Kai. Not them, not me—*you.*"

The tension shifted, the murmurs fading into a stillness that felt alive, electric. Kai unclenched his fists, his sketchpad sliding open as if drawn by instinct. Lena smoothed out her napkin, her shoulders straightening as she traced the smudged lines of her poem. Tariq flipped his laptop open, the screen flickering to life with a soft hum. The newer faces exchanged glances, some nodding, others hesitating but staying put. Ray exhaled, relief mingling with pride. The circle wasn't whole yet, but it wasn't broken either—at least not entirely.

Leila's Guilt And Growth

The meeting ended with tentative agreements—Kai promising to sketch something new, Lena vowing to read next week, Tariq muttering about a coding tweak—but Ray knew the doubt lingered, a shadow the enforcers had planted too deep to uproot in one night. As the teens filtered out into the drizzle-soaked streets, Leila slipped in through the back door, her curly hair damp and clinging to her face, her sharp eyes shadowed with a guilt Ray recognized from their café confrontation weeks ago. She carried a stack of the flyers under her arm, their accusing words peeking out like a wound she couldn't hide.

"You're late," Ray said, forcing a grin to lighten the weight pressing against his ribs, but it faltered as she dropped the stack onto the table with a heavy thud. The papers fanned out, *Ray Carter's Lies* glaring up at him in stark black ink, the red circle around his face a silent threat.

"I found these," she said, her voice low and trembling, a mix of fury and shame threading through it. "All over the neighbourhood—streets, lampposts, taped to shop windows. I tried to rip them down, Ray, but they're everywhere. And it's my fault."

Ray frowned, picking up a flyer, its edges curled from the rain, the ink smudged but legible. "What are you talking about?"

She crossed her arms, her gaze dropping to the floor as if she couldn't bear to meet his eyes. "Back when they came to me—those men in suits—I told you I fed them info to keep them off your back. I thought I was protecting you, playing their game so they wouldn't hurt you. But they're using it now. Twisting it." She pointed to the flyer, her hand shaking. "Those words— 'delusions,' 'lies'—some of them are mine. From what I wrote to keep them away. I gave them the ammunition, Ray, and now they're turning it on you, on the kids."

Her confession crashed over him like a wave, dragging up the sting of her earlier betrayal—the letter she'd written detailing his dreams, handed to the enforcers in a desperate bid to shield him. He'd forgiven her then, reframed it as a test he'd passed, but this—this was a deeper cut, a wound reopened by the sight of her words weaponized against everything he'd built. Anger flared, hot and jagged, urging him to snap, to demand how she could've been so blind. But he caught it, held it, let it pass through him like smoke on the wind. Elias's lesson anchored him: *You control your reaction.*

"Leila," he said, his voice steady despite the ache in his chest, "that's over. You told me, we discussed it, we have moved past it. This isn't on you."

"No, it's not over," she snapped, her eyes flashing as they finally met his, glistening with unshed tears. "I didn't just give them facts—I gave them my doubts, my stupid fears about you losing yourself in this. They're using my words to make Kai question you, to make Lena afraid. I should've seen it, Ray—I should've known they'd twist it like this."

Her voice broke, the guilt she'd buried since Evan's death spilling out in a rush—a grief she'd turned into a vow to save Ray, now twisted into a weapon against them both. Ray stepped closer, resting a hand on her shoulder, the contact grounding her as she'd grounded him so many times before. "You couldn't have known Leila," he said, his tone firm but gentle. "They're not winning because of you—they're scared because of what we're doing. You didn't start this fire; they did. And you're not the one tearing it down—I am, by keeping it alive."

Leila's breath shuddered, her shoulders slumping as the fight drained out of her. "I can't lose you, Ray," she whispered, her voice raw with a fear she rarely let show. "Not like Evan. Not after everything." Her eyes welled up.

"You won't," he promised, his grip tightening, a quiet vow in the gesture. "We're in this together—always have been. They can twist your words, but they can't twist us—not unless we let them."

She exhaled, a shaky breath that carried years of buried pain, and wiped her eyes with the back of her hand. The fire returned, flickering but growing, as she straightened. "Okay," she said, her voice steadying. "So, what do we do about them?"

Ray grinned, a spark of defiance igniting within him, chasing away the lingering sting. "We keep going. We show them—everyone—what we're made of. They want doubt? We'll give them certainty."

Her smile broke through, small but fierce, a mirror of the strength they'd forged together. "You're impossible, you know that?"

"Learned from the best," he shot back, and for a moment, the shadows lifted, their bond a shield against the storm brewing outside. She nodded, gathering the flyers into a messy pile, her movements purposeful now—a silent promise to fight alongside him, to rewrite her guilt into resolve.

The Price Of Defiance

The rooftop loomed under a sky bruised with clouds, its rusted door a silent sentinel as Ray climbed the stairs, Leila at his side. The hum pulsed stronger now, a low roar threading through the night, shadows shifting along the edges of his vision like restless ghosts. Elias waited near the railing, his silver hair catching the faint glow of the city, his sharp eyes glinting with a mix of pride and weariness as they approached.

"You're still standing," Elias said, his voice warm but edged with a gravity that set Ray's nerves alight. "That's more than most manage."

Ray handed him a flyer, its crumpled paper stark against the night. "They're hitting us where it hurts the most. The kids—my mentees—my circle of trust, they're doubting everything now. They are being weakened."

Elias unfolded it, his expression darkening as he scanned the words—Leila's words, twisted into a weapon. "They're clever," he muttered, tossing it aside to flutter into the darkness below. "They don't need to erase you if they can break what sustains you."

Leila crossed her arms, her voice sharp with lingering pain. "They're using me to do it—my mistakes, my words. How do we fight that?"

Elias's gaze softened, shifting to her with a rare tenderness. "You're here, Leila—that's how. Seeing your flaws turned against you is the cost of this path. But it's also your strength. You've faced it, owned it. They can't use what you've already claimed."

Ray stepped closer, his mind churning with questions the night couldn't silence. "What's it cost you, Elias? You've guided us, warned us, but you've never said what you've given up."

Elias exhaled, his shoulders sagging slightly as he turned to the skyline, his voice dropping to a low, heavy cadence. "Everything," he said, the word a stone sinking into still the water. "I told you about Mara—my partner, the one they erased. But that was just the end of it. Before that, I had a life—family, a sister who laughed like the world couldn't touch her, friends who filled quiet nights with stories. When I saw the framework, when I leapt and landed beyond their reach, I lost it all—not because they took it, but because I couldn't go back. Seeing the truth isolates you, Ray. It burns the bridges you didn't know you'd need in the future. Comfort, safety, the people you love—it's all ash when you choose this."

Ray's chest tightened, the weight of Elias's sacrifice crashing over him like a tide. He'd lost Mara to the enforcers' erasure, but the rest—*the life he'd left behind—had been a choice, a price paid willingly* to defy the framework. "And you think that's waiting for us?" he asked, his voice steady despite the ache.

"I think it's already begun," Elias said, glancing at Leila, then back to Ray. "You've lost the luxury of ignorance—both of you. The enforcers will keep coming, through doubt, through betrayal, through every crack they can widen. *But the cost isn't just what you lose—it's what you gain, what you become.* You've seen what they fear: a mind that won't bow, a will that rewrites their game. That's worth more than safety ever could be."

Leila frowned, her voice cutting through the quiet. "So, we just keep paying? Losing more every time they push?"

"No," Elias said, his tone hardening with resolve. "*You keep choosing.* Every flyer they spread, every doubt they sow—it's a chance to prove them wrong, to show the kids what you've shown me. *The cost isn't the end—it's the price of freedom.* I paid it. Mara paid it. Now, it's your turn to decide if it's worth it."

Ray clenched his fists, the fire in his chest blazing brighter than the city below. He thought of Kai's wavering trust, Lena's trembling courage, Tariq's silent potential—the sparks he'd lit, now flickering under the enforcers' shadow. He thought of Leila's guilt, her strength reborn in this moment. The cost was steep—trust fractured, peace shattered, a life forever altered—but it was his to bear. "They've already lost," he said, meeting Elias's gaze, his voice ringing with defiance. "I'm not giving up—not on this, not on them."

Elias's smile was faint but fierce, pride glinting in his eyes like a beacon. "Good. Because the *real fight isn't just surviving—it's thriving.* They want you broken. Show them unbreakable."

The hum pulsed again, shadows shifting along the rooftop's edge—a whisper of the enforcers' next move, a challenge lurking in the dark. Ray squared his shoulders, Leila at his side, Elias's truth a torch lighting the path ahead. The cost of seeing was heavy—doubt, guilt, sacrifice—but *it was a price he'd pay willingly.* He'd face it, not with fear, but with the power he'd claimed: belief.

"Let's go," he said, stepping toward the stairwell, his voice a quiet thunder. "We've got work to do."

The night stretched before them, alive with challenge and possibilities—a world they'd fight for, together.

Chapter - 16
Leap Of Courage

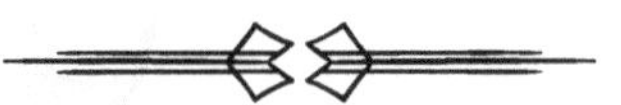

"Courage is not the absence of fear, but doing what needs to be done despite having the fear."

— **Unknown**

The Edge Of Doubt

Ray stood at the edge of the community centre's rooftop, the city of 2042 sprawling beneath him like a restless sea of light and shadow. The wind bit at his skin, tugging at his jacket and tousling his messy black hair, a cold reminder of the height that loomed before him. His boots grazed the concrete lip, the faint crunch of gravel underfoot swallowed by the distant hum of drones weaving through the night sky. His hands gripped the rusted railing, the metal cool and unyielding against his palms, anchoring him as his mind teetered on a precipice far more treacherous than the one below.

The alley waited, a shadowed maw stretching into the darkness, its depths promising either oblivion or revelation. His breath came in shallow bursts, fogging in the frigid air, each exhale a battle against the doubt clawing at his chest. He'd leapt before—through the rooftop door into alternate realities, off this very edge to test his belief—but those had been guided, orchestrated by Elias's cryptic lessons. This was different. This was his choice, unprompted, a leap not just of body but of will. The key from Elias's notebook rested heavy in his pocket, its edges worn smooth by his restless fingers, a silent talisman of the power he'd claimed—and the risk he now faced.

Leila stood a few paces behind, her curly hair dancing in the breeze, her sharp brown eyes fixed on him with an intensity that made his heart ache. She didn't speak, didn't push—not yet—but her presence was a tether, a lifeline pulling him back from the abyss of his own thoughts. The rooftop wasn't just a physical space tonight; it was a crucible, a threshold between the Ray who'd let life happen to him and the Ray who might dare to shape it. He'd faced Zane without reacting, forgiven Leila's betrayal, bent reality to escape the enforcers' sterile prison. But this—this leap—felt like the culmination of it all, a test of courage he couldn't back away from.

His throat tightened, a cocktail of fear and exhilaration surging through him. Below, the city pulsed with life— hover-cars gliding silently, thought-responsive billboards flickering with ads tailored to the minds below. He'd escaped those enforcers, rewritten their trap with his belief, but their threat lingered like a shadow he couldn't shake. *You've gone too far. Turn back.* The note they'd left burned in his memory, a warning he'd answered with defiance: *You can't stop what's already begun.* But what if he was wrong? What if this leap didn't prove his power but exposed its limits? What if he fell—not into a new reality, but into nothing?

"You're overthinking it again," Leila said, her voice slicing through the wind like a knife through fog. She stepped closer, her boots scuffing the concrete, her arms crossed in a challenge that masked her concern. "You've been staring at that drop for ages. What's stopping you?"

Ray turned to her, his dark eyes searching hers for the certainty she always carried like a shield. "What if I'm not enough?" he said, his voice raw, quieter than he'd intended. "What if I jump, and it's just... over? No shift, no proof—just a fall?"

Leila's lips pressed into a thin line, her gaze softening but unyielding. "And what if you don't jump? What if you stay here, stuck, letting that question eat you alive? You've already come this far, Ray—don't tell me you're going let fear win now."

Her words stung, not because they were harsh, but because they echoed the truth he'd been dodging. He'd spent years letting fear dictate his steps—fear of failure, of rejection, of being less than he could be. It had kept him small, a shadow drifting through a life he didn't claim. But the shifts, the tests, Elias's lessons—they'd cracked that shell, let light seep into the places he'd kept dark. He wasn't that Ray anymore. Or he didn't have to be.

"I don't know what's down there," he admitted, his hands tightening on the railing until his knuckles whitened. "What if I can't control it? What if I lose everything— everything I've built?"

Leila stepped beside him, her shoulder brushing his, her warmth cutting through the chill. "You won't lose it," she said, her tone softer now, laced with a depth that steadied him. "You've got me here, Ray. And I'm not letting you fall apart—not after all this. You've faced worse than a drop. You've faced yourself."

Leila's Anchor

Her words pierced him, a lifeline he hadn't realized he needed until it was there. Ray glanced at her, caught off guard by the vulnerability threading through her voice. Leila was a storm—fierce, relentless, a force that swept him along when he couldn't move himself. But now, in the dim glow of the rooftop, he saw something more—the cracks beneath her resolve, the weight she carried that she rarely let slip.

"Why do you keep doing this?" he asked, the question spilling out before he could stop it. "Pushing me, dragging me out of my head—why does it matter to you so much?"

She looked away, her gaze drifting to the city below, her fingers tightening around her arms as if to hold herself together. For a moment, he thought she wouldn't answer, that she'd deflect with a quip or a challenge as she always did. Then she exhaled, a shaky breath that carried a pain he hadn't fully grasped until now.

"Because I couldn't save Evan," she said, her voice barely audible, trembling with a grief she'd buried deep. "My brother—he was like you, Ray. Lost, doubting, trapped in his own head. He'd sit for hours, staring at nothing, telling me the world didn't care, that nothing he did would change it. I tried to pull him out—tried to make him see what I saw in him—but I was too late. He got caught up in drugs, in despair, and one night... I found him on the floor, gone. Cold. I couldn't bring him back."

Ray's chest tightened, a lump rising in his throat as her words sank in. He'd known she'd lost someone—pieced it together from stray comments, from the way her eyes darkened sometimes—but not this. Not the raw, jagged truth of it. All those nights she'd hauled him to the bookstore, pushed him to face the world, he'd thought it was just her stubbornness, her need to fix things. But it was more—a wound turned into a vow, a refusal to let another light fade.

"I didn't see it then," she continued, her voice steadying but thick with emotion. "How much he needed someone to believe in him when he couldn't. When I found you on that rooftop two years ago, I saw him—saw the same emptiness, the same questions. I swore I wouldn't let it happen again. You're not Evan, Ray, but you've got that same spark he lost. I can't—I won't—watch it go out."

Her confession hung between them, a fragile thread binding their fates. Ray's throat burned, not just for her pain but for the mirror it held to his own—those years he'd drifted, expecting nothing, letting the world confirm his worthlessness. He reached out, resting a hand on her arm, the contact a silent promise. "I'm not going anywhere," he said, his voice hoarse but firm. "Not like that."

Leila's eyes glistened, but she blinked the tears away, a faint smile breaking through. "Good. Then leap, you stubborn idiot. Show me what you've got—what I've always known you had."

Her belief in him—fierce, unwavering—ignited something deep within Ray, a warmth that chased away the cold tendrils of doubt. She wasn't just his anchor; she was his spark, the one who'd seen him when he couldn't see himself. He turned back to the edge, her words a fire in his veins, pushing him past the fear that had held him back for too long.

Fear Versus Hope

The city lights blurred into a sea of possibility below, their glow a stark contrast to the darkness of the alley. Fear gnawed at him, vivid and visceral, painting images that made his stomach churn. He saw himself falling—crashing into the pavement, his body broken and still, the key useless in his pocket as the enforcers' hollow laughter echoed from the void. He saw their distorted forms emerging from the shadows, proving his belief was a delusion, his power a fleeting dream. Failure loomed, a spectre he'd known too well, whispering that he'd never been enough, that this leap would be his end.

But then hope flickered—a brighter, fiercer flame cutting through the gloom. What if he didn't fall? What if he leapt and the world bent to meet him, as it had through the door, as it had in the enforcers' prison? He pictured landing—not broken, but whole—his boots hitting the ground with a force that rippled outward, reshaping the alley, the city, the reality he claimed as his own. He saw himself not as a victim of gravity, but as its master, belief carrying him where doubt never could. Elias's voice echoed: *Your thoughts are more powerful than you realize.* He'd rewritten coffee cups, faced bullies, escaped erasure—why not this?

The two visions battled within him—failure's icy grip versus transformation's warm pull. His breath steadied, his hands unclenching as he let fear flow through him, not over him. He wasn't leaping blind. He was leaping with intent, with faith in the man he'd become. The key in his pocket wasn't just a tool—it was a symbol of his agency, his choice. He didn't need Elias to guide him this time. He'd guide himself.

"Okay," he said, more to himself than Leila, his voice cutting through the wind. "Let's see what I can do."

Elias's Wisdom

Footsteps echoed from the stairwell—slow, deliberate, a rhythm Ray knew like his own heartbeat. He turned, expecting an empty rooftop, but Elias emerged from the shadows, his silver hair glinting under the faint glow of a flickering bulb. His presence was a jolt, a steadying force amidst the chaos of Ray's thoughts. He stopped a few feet away, hands in his pockets, his sharp eyes studying Ray with a mix of curiosity and expectation.

"You're here," Ray said, surprise mingling with relief, his voice rough from the tension.

Elias tilted his head, a faint smirk tugging at his lips. "Did you think I'd miss this?"

Ray swallowed, the weight of Elias's gaze pushing him to speak. "I don't know if I can do it—not like before. That was different. This… this is just me."

Elias stepped closer, his voice low but resonant, cutting through the wind like a blade through silence. "It's always been just you, Ray. Every shift, every test—it's been your mind, your will. The doors, the leaps—they were just tools to show you what's already there." He tapped his temple, his eyes locking onto Ray's with an intensity that burned. "Reality's fluid—it bends to what you hold true. I learned that the hard way."

Ray frowned, catching the shift in Elias's tone—a crack in the calm, a glimpse of something deeper. "What do you mean?"

Elias's gaze drifted to the horizon, a shadow passing over his face, his voice softening with the weight of memory. "Years ago, I stood where you are—on a rooftop, different city, same edge. I'd lost everything—my sister, my home—because I believed the world was a fixed thing, a machine I couldn't touch. I leapt, expecting it to end me. But I didn't fall—not like I thought. I landed somewhere else, a reality I'd shaped without knowing, a place where I wasn't broken. It terrified me, Ray, but it taught me something: belief isn't a wish—it's a force. I've been running from that truth ever since, guiding others to face it instead. You're the first who's come this far."

Ray's breath caught, the story sinking into him like roots into soil. Elias wasn't just a mentor—he was a survivor, a man who'd leapt into the unknown and lived, who'd seen the edges of reality Ray was only beginning to grasp. "So, this works?" he asked, his voice steadier now, bolstered by Elias's confession. "If I believe it?"

Elias nodded, his smirk softening into something warmer, a rare flicker of vulnerability breaking through. "It always has. The question isn't whether it works—it's what you believe and how intensely you believe it. Failure, or something more?"

Ray turned back to the edge, Elias's words igniting the hope he'd clung to, fanning it into a blaze. He saw it now—the leap wasn't about the fall; it was about the landing, about choosing what came next. He pulled the key from his pocket, holding it up to the light, its surface catching the city's glow like a promise. "Something more," he said, slipping it back into his jacket, the decision settling over him like armour.

Elias stepped back, giving him space, his voice a quiet challenge. "Then show me."

The Leap

Ray faced the drop, his heart pounding but his mind clear, a clarity cutting through the storm of doubt. Leila's hand brushed his arm, a final nudge of faith, her warmth a steady pulse against the cold. "You've got this," she whispered, her voice a lifeline he didn't need to clutch—just knowing it was there was enough.

He took a deep breath, letting the city's hum fill him, a symphony of life he'd learned to shape. Fear lingered, a faint echo at the edges of his thoughts, but hope drowned it out, a roar that silenced the whispers of failure. He didn't need to know the exact outcome—only that he'd define it. His legs tensed, his body coiling with intent, and then he leapt.

The wind roared past, a howl that swallowed his gasp as the rooftop vanished above him. His stomach flipped, the alley rushing up to meet him in a blur of shadow and light, but he didn't flinch. He focused—on landing, on bending the fall to his will, on claiming this moment as his own. The air thickened, resisting gravity's pull, slowing his descent as if the universe itself bent to his command. His boots hit the ground—not with a crash, but with a soft thud, the pavement rippling faintly beneath him like water settling after a stone's drop.

He stood, unharmed, no pain, not even a scratch. Ray felt the adrenaline surging through him as a laugh—raw, exultant—burst from his throat, echoing off the alley walls. He'd done it—not through a door, not guided by Elias, but by his own courage, his own belief. He looked up, Leila leaning over the edge, her grin wide and triumphant, Elias beside her, his nod a silent affirmation. The city loomed around him, solid and alive, its heartbeat syncing with his own.

Ray's chest heaved, but the fire within him burned brighter than ever. He'd leapt into the unknown, faced the fear that had once defined him, and landed not just alive but transformed. The enforcers' threats, the hum pulsing faintly in the distance—they didn't matter. Not now, not anymore. He'd proven something tonight—to himself, to Leila, to Elias, to the shadows that watched: he was no longer a pawn in their game. He was a force not just to recon with but someone they couldn't contain.

The alley stretched before him, a path he'd carved with his own will. He didn't know what lay ahead—the enforcers' next move, the mysteries Elias hinted at—but he knew one thing: he was ready. Not just to survive, but to create and thrive. To leap again, and again, until the world matched the man he'd become.

"Let them watch," he muttered, grinning into the night as he stepped forward, the city unfolding around him like a promise he'd keep.

Chapter - 17
The Turning Point

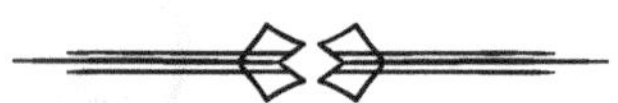

"In the midst of chaos, there is also opportunity."

— **Sun Tzu.**

The city sprawled beneath a bruised purple sky, its lights flickering like the last gasps of a dying star. Ray Carter walked its streets alone, his breath misting in the unseasonably cold air. His hands were stuffed deep into the pockets of his worn jacket, fingers brushing against the crumpled edge of a note he'd found slipped under his apartment door earlier that day: *"Be careful what you think. They are watching."* Unsigned. Unexplained. Yet it carried a weight that gnawed at him, a splinter lodged beneath his skin.

He had come so far. The book—his book—was a beacon now, its words rippling through lives he'd never even touched. His mentorship program thrived, a testament to the power of collective growth, collective consciousness. He had rewritten his reality, shaped it with intention, just as Elias had taught him. Perception was his tool, resilience his armour, self-belief his power. He had believed, truly believed, that once he grasped these truths, the doubts would fade, the path would clear, and the chaos of his old life would dissolve into memory.

He had been wrong.

The air felt heavy tonight, thick with an unspoken warning. The city, his city, no longer seemed like a canvas he painted with his thoughts. It felt like a mirror turned inward, reflecting something he couldn't yet name. Elias had been gone for weeks—vanished without a word, leaving Ray to navigate this newfound purpose, *alone.* The absence gnawed at him, a quiet ache that grew louder with each unanswered question. Where was the man who had set him on this path? And why did it feel like the world was holding its breath?

Ray tilted his head back, staring at the sky. No stars tonight—just a vast, empty expanse that pressed down like a judgment. He thought of Elias's voice, calm and steady: *"Your world is the result of what you focus on."* If that was true, then what was he focusing on now to summon this unease? Was it doubt creeping back, or something more?

The note crinkled in his pocket. *They are watching.* Who? And why now, when he finally felt like he was becoming the person he was meant to be? His steps slowed as he reached the edge of a familiar alley, its shadows stretching toward him like fingers. He exhaled sharply, trying to shake the feeling. He was stronger now—resilient. Situations only had power if he let them. He could choose his response.

But then the streetlamp above him flickered. Once. Twice. A low hum vibrated through the pavement, barely audible but enough to set his nerves on edge. Ray froze, his gaze darting around. The alley was empty, the street silent except for the distant rumble of traffic. Yet the hum grew louder, a pulse that seemed to sync with his heartbeat.

"Get a grip," he muttered to himself, rubbing his temples. Exhaustion, that's all it was. Too many late nights, too many speeches, too many expectations piling up. He turned to keep walking, but a flicker of movement caught his eye—a shadow shifting where no shadow should be.

Ray's breath hitched. He squinted into the darkness, his rational mind wrestling with the instinct clawing at his chest. It was nothing. A trick of the light. Perception, right? He shaped his reality. He took a step forward, forcing calm into his voice. "Who's there?"

Silence answered him. Then, a whisper—so faint it could have been the wind: *"You are close."*

The words sent a jolt through him, sharp and electric. He spun around, scanning the empty street. No one. Nothing. His heart pounded against his ribs, a frantic rhythm he couldn't control. He stumbled back, his shoulder brushing the rough brick of the alley wall. The note burned in his pocket. *They are watching.* Was this what it meant? Was someone—or something—testing him?

He needed answers. And there was only one place he could think to find them.

The rooftop loomed ahead, a silhouette against the bruised sky. Ray climbed the stairs two at a time, his boots echoing in the narrow stairwell. The familiar ache of those steps tugged at him—memories of the night he'd first followed Elias here, the night he'd stepped through a door and into a truth he couldn't unsee. That moment had been the spark, the turning point that set everything in motion. Maybe it still held the key.

The door creaked as he pushed it open, a gust of frigid wind slapping his face. The city stretched out below, its lights a constellation of lives he now felt tethered to. He stepped onto the rooftop, his breath clouding in the air, and stopped short.

Elias was there.

He stood at the edge, his back to Ray, silver hair catching the faint glow of the skyline. He didn't turn, didn't move, as if carved from the night itself. Relief flooded Ray, followed swiftly by a wave of unease. Something was wrong. The air around Elias felt... hollow, devoid of the quiet strength Ray had come to rely on.

"Elias?" Ray's voice trembled despite his effort to steady it.

Slowly, Elias turned. Ray's stomach dropped. Those eyes—once sharp with wisdom, alive with purpose—were dull, empty. A shadow of the man he'd known stared back at him, and for a moment, Ray couldn't breathe.

"You shouldn't have come here," Elias said, his voice flat, lifeless.

Ray took a cautious step forward, hands clenching at his sides. "What's happening? Where have you been? I've been looking for you—everyone has. And then this—" He pulled the note from his pocket, holding it up. "What does it mean?"

Elias tilted his head, studying him with an unnerving detachment. "You're starting to see it, aren't you?"

"See *what*?" Ray's frustration boiled over, his voice rising. "I've been trying to live what you taught me—to shape my world, to choose my reactions. But now it feels like something's pushing back. Like I'm not in control anymore."

A faint smile flickered across Elias's lips, but it held no warmth. "The illusion is breaking. And they don't like that."

Ray's pulse thundered in his ears. "Who's 'they'? You keep talking in riddles—give me something real!"

Before Elias could respond, the rooftop door slammed open with a force that rattled the hinges. Ray whipped around, his heart lurching as two figures emerged from the stairwell shadows. Men in dark suits, their movements too precise, too fluid—almost mechanical. Their eyes glinted like glass under the dim light, unblinking and cold.

Instinct screamed at Ray to run, but his feet stayed rooted. He glanced back at Elias, who hadn't moved, his expression unreadable. "Elias—what—."

"They've been waiting," Elias interrupted, his voice cutting through the tension like a blade. "Waiting for you to reach this point. To see beyond what you were meant to see."

The taller of the two figures stepped forward, his voice smooth and emotionless. "Mr. Carter, we need you to come with us."

Ray's mind raced. Every lesson Elias had drilled into him flared to life: *Situations only have power if you react to them.* He could feel the fear clawing at him, the urge to bolt, to fight, to demand answers. But he forced himself to breathe, to focus. He wouldn't let them dictate this moment.

"Who are you?" he asked, his tone steady despite the tremble in his hands.

The shorter figure tilted his head, a faint smirk tugging at his lips. "That's not your concern. Not yet."

Ray's jaw tightened. "I'm not going anywhere until I understand what's happening."

Elias spoke again, his voice softer now, almost regretful. "You've pushed the boundaries, Ray. You've seen how perception shapes reality—but you've only scratched the surface. They're here because you're waking up."

"Waking up to what?" Ray snapped, his patience fraying.

The taller figure took another step, closing the distance. "Enough questions. This ends now."

Adrenaline surged through Ray like wildfire. He didn't know who these men were, what they wanted, or why Elias seemed so different—but he knew one thing: he wouldn't surrender control. Not after everything he'd fought to become.

He turned and bolted toward the edge of the rooftop.

"Stop!" the taller figure shouted, but Ray didn't hesitate.

The city loomed below, a dizzying drop that should have paralyzed him with fear. But fear was a choice, and he refused it. He leaped, the wind roaring in his ears, his body weightless for one terrifying, exhilarating moment. He didn't know what would happen—whether he'd hit the pavement or something else—but he trusted the lessons he'd learned. Perception was his power. He could shape this.

Darkness swallowed him.

When awareness returned, it came in fragments—sharp pain in his ribs, the cold bite of pavement beneath him, the distant wail of sirens. Ray groaned, forcing his eyes open. He wasn't on the rooftop anymore, but he wasn't dead either. He lay in an alley, the same one he'd passed earlier, its walls towering around him like sentinels.

He pushed himself up, wincing as his bruised body protested. The jump should have killed him. Yet here he was, alive, intact. Had he shaped this outcome? Had his belief carried him through?

Footsteps echoed behind him. Ray tensed, turning to see Elias emerging from the shadows, his expression no longer hollow but urgent.

"You're still here," Elias said, a flicker of relief in his voice.

Ray staggered to his feet, anger and confusion warring inside him. "What the hell is going on, Elias? Who were those men? Why did you let them—"

"They're not men," Elias interrupted, his gaze darting to the rooftops above. "They're enforcers. Guardians of the framework you've started to unravel."

"Framework?" Ray's mind spun. "You mean reality?"

Elias nodded grimly. "The reality you've been shaping— it's not yours alone. It's part of something bigger, something they control. And you're threatening it."

Ray's knees buckled, the weight of the words crashing over him. All this time, he'd thought he was mastering his world, bending it to his will. But what if he'd only been scratching at the surface of a deeper truth—one someone, or something, didn't want him to see?

"Why me?" he whispered.

Elias stepped closer, his eyes locking onto Ray's. "Because you stopped reacting and started choosing. Because you proved the mind's power goes beyond what they expected. You're a glitch, Ray—a fragment they can't predict."

A low hum vibrated through the alley again, louder this time, the shadows twisting unnaturally. Elias grabbed Ray's arm. "We need to move. They're coming back."

Ray pulled free, planting his feet. "No. I'm done running. If they want me, they'll have to face me."

Elias's eyes widened, then softened with something like pride. "Then you're ready."

"For what?"

Elias's voice dropped to a whisper. "To fight for the truth."

The hum crescendoed, the air crackling with energy. Ray turned, his heart steady despite the chaos. Whatever came next—whatever *they* were—he wouldn't let them take his power. He'd spent too long believing he was powerless to surrender now.

The shadows parted, and the figures returned—more this time, their forms shifting, distorting reality itself. Ray squared his shoulders, his mind racing but clear.

This was the turning point.

Not just for him, but for everything.

Chapter - 18
The Reckoning

*"Sometimes, the only way forward is
to leap into the unknown."*

— Anonymous

Ray's consciousness flickered like a candle caught in a storm, wavering between darkness and dim awareness. His body felt anchored, heavy as if gravity itself had thickened around him, pinning him to an unseen surface. Pain pulsed faintly through his limbs—a dull reminder that he was still alive, still tethered to existence. But where? The last thing he remembered was the rooftop, the cold wind biting his face, the figures in dark suits closing in, and then—nothing. A void. A fall.

He forced his eyes open, blinking against a harsh, flickering light. The world came into focus slowly, jagged edges resolving into something sterile and unfamiliar. No city skyline stretched before him. No stars pierced the night. Instead, he found himself in a room—metallic, bare, suffocating in its simplicity. The walls gleamed with a cold sheen, reflecting the erratic buzz of a single overhead bulb. No windows. No door that he could see. Just a chair in the centre of the room, and sitting in it—a figure that made his stomach lurch.

It was him.

Ray's breath caught, sharp and ragged. He squinted, his mind scrambling to make sense of the sight. The figure mirrored his posture, his dishevelled black hair, his worn jacket—but it didn't move. He tilted his head; the reflection stayed still. He raised a hand; the figure remained frozen, staring back with hollow eyes. It wasn't a mirror. It was something else—a shadow of himself, a mockery of who he was. Panic clawed at his chest, but he swallowed it down, forcing his thoughts to steady.

Perception shapes reality, he reminded himself. Whatever this was, he wouldn't let it unravel him.

The air shifted, a faint creak cutting through the silence. A seam appeared in the seamless wall, widening into a door. Two figures stepped through—the men from the rooftop. Their suits were pristine, their movements too smooth, too precise, like machines wrapped in human skin. The taller one, with sharp cheekbones and a gaze that pierced like a blade, spoke first.

"Mr. Carter," he said, his voice a low hum that vibrated through the room. "You've seen too much."

Ray pushed himself upright, ignoring the ache in his bones. His hands trembled, but he clenched them into fists, anchoring himself. "Where am I? What do you want?"

The shorter man, his face softer but no less menacing, stepped forward and placed a sleek tablet on the table that had materialized between them. His fingers brushed the screen, and it flickered to life. A video began to play— grainy at first, then sharpening into clarity. Ray's breath hitched as he watched himself: walking the city streets, speaking at book signings, laughing with Leila over coffee. Moments he'd lived, moments that had defined his transformation, all captured in cold, unblinking detail. Every step, every word, every choice—monitored.

"You think your thoughts shape reality," the taller man said, his tone devoid of emotion. "But what if reality has been shaping you?"

Ray's pulse thundered in his ears. He forced his voice to steady, though it cracked at the edges. "Who are you? What is this place?"

The shorter man smirked, a flicker of amusement breaking his otherwise impassive mask. "We are the ones who ensure people like you don't see beyond the veil. The ones who keep the world predictable."

Ray's mind raced, fragments of Elias's lessons colliding with this new, incomprehensible threat. *The world is not something that happens to you. It's something you create.* But these men—they spoke as if his reality, his power, was a threat to something larger. Something orchestrated.

"You're saying the world isn't what it seems?" he asked, his voice sharper now, defiance cutting through the fear.

The shorter man leaned forward, his glass-like eyes glinting under the flickering light. "Let's just say your belief that perception shapes reality is more dangerous than you think."

Ray's jaw tightened. Dangerous—to whom? He'd spent months unravelling the truth, learning to wield his mind like a tool, bending the world to reflect his choices. He'd leapt from rooftops, faced betrayal, rewritten his existence—all because he believed he could. And now these men, these *things*, wanted to cage that power?

"What do you want from me?" he demanded, his gaze darting between them.

The taller man slid off the table's edge where he'd perched, his movements fluid and deliberate. "A choice," he said. "You can forget all of this—return to your life, live in comfort, and never question what you saw. Or you keep going, and face the consequences."

The word *consequences* hung in the air like a guillotine blade. Ray's heart pounded, a rhythm of defiance and dread. He had tasted freedom. He'd come too far to retreat—too far to let fear dictate his path again. He thought of Leila's unwavering belief in him, of Elias's cryptic guidance, of the countless lives his words had touched. Turning back meant erasing that, surrendering the man he'd become. But pressing forward—what did that mean? What could they do to him? What price he will have to pay?

"And if I refuse?" he asked, his voice low but steady.

The shorter man's smile widened, cold and predatory. "Then you cease to exist."

A chill slithered down Ray's spine, prickling his skin. "You mean you'll kill me?"

"No, we don't have to do that. There are better ways of handling things…. like you" the taller man said, his tone almost casual as he adjusted his cuff. "You will simply… no longer be part of this world's equation. No one will remember you as if you never existed."

Ray's knees weakened, but he locked them in place. Not death, but erasure. A void where he'd been—a reality without Ray Carter. The weight of it pressed against his chest, threatening to crush him. He could feel the old Ray clawing to the surface—the one who'd stood on rooftops contemplating nothingness, the one who'd let fear rule him. But that Ray was gone. He'd buried him with every choice, every leap into the unknown.

He closed his eyes, drawing a slow, deliberate breath. Elias's voice echoed in his mind: *People and situations have no power unless you let them.* This room, these men, this threat—they were real, but their hold over him wasn't. *He could choose.* He always could.

When he opened his eyes, a spark of clarity ignited within him. If reality bent to perception, then he could bend this moment too. He didn't need to fight them with fists or words—he could fight them with belief.

"I'm not afraid of you," he said, his voice cutting through the sterile air. "You don't control me."

The taller man's expression faltered, a flicker of unease breaking his composure. "You don't understand what you're—"

"I don't need to," Ray interrupted, stepping forward. "You think you can erase me? You think you can take away what I've built? I've rewritten my world before. I'll do it again."

The room trembled—a subtle vibration at first, then a ripple that warped the metallic walls like water disturbed by a stone. The men exchanged a glance, their calm facades cracking. Ray focused harder, picturing the city streets, the rooftop, the life he'd claimed as his own. The air thickened, the flickering light stuttering as if caught in a glitch.

"He's breaking it—!" the shorter man shouted, lunging for the tablet.

Ray moved faster. He snatched the device and smashed it against the table, the screen shattering into a spiderweb of cracks. The room fractured with it—walls splintering like glass, the floor tilting beneath his feet. The men's forms flickered, their outlines dissolving into static.

And then he was falling.

Darkness swallowed him, a rush of wind roaring in his ears. His stomach flipped, but he didn't resist. He'd leapt before—into uncertainty, into possibility—and survived. This was no different. He pictured the alley, the city's heartbeat, the freedom he'd fought for. If perception was his power, then he'd land where he chose.

Light exploded around him, sharp and blinding. He hit the ground hard, pavement biting into his palms as he gasped for air. The cold night wrapped around him, familiar and alive. He was back—sprawled in the alley where he'd faced Elias moments before the rooftop chaos. His chest heaved, adrenaline surging, but a grin tugged at his lips. He'd done it. He'd shaped the outcome, yet again.

Footsteps echoed behind him. Ray tensed, scrambling to his feet, ready to face the suited men again. But it wasn't them.

Elias emerged from the shadows, his silver hair glinting under a streetlamp. His eyes were no longer dull—they burned with urgency, with pride. "You're still here," he said, a note of relief softening his voice.

Ray wiped a trickle of blood from his lip, his grin widening despite the ache in his ribs. "Did you doubt me?"

Elias chuckled, a rare sound that cut through the tension. "Not for a moment. But they did."

Ray glanced up at the rooftop, its silhouette looming against the bruised sky. "They're not done with me, are they?"

"No," Elias said, stepping closer. "They won't let you go so easily. You've seen the edges of their framework—pushed beyond what they normally allow. They'll regroup, recalibrate. But you've proven something tonight."

Ray met his gaze, steady despite the exhaustion weighing him down. "What's that?"

"That you're stronger than they think," Elias said. "Stronger than their control. You didn't just escape—you rewrote the rules."

Ray exhaled, the weight of those words settling over him. He'd leapt into the unknown, not knowing if he'd survive, and emerged not just alive but victorious. The men—or whatever they were—had tried to strip him of his power, his existence. But they'd failed. *Because he'd chosen to fight*, not with fists or weapons, but *with the one thing they couldn't take: his mind.*

There is only one thing in this world which can always be under your control and that is your mind, how do you think. And Ray did just that, he kept his mind in his control even when his very existence was under credible threat.

"So, what now?" he asked, brushing dirt from his jacket. "They'll come back. What do I do?"

Elias smirked, a glint of mischief in his eyes. "You keep going. You keep choosing. They thrive on predictability—on people who react instead of create. But you? You're a variable they can't predict, can't solve."

Ray nodded, the fire in his chest flaring brighter. He thought of the note from earlier—*They are watching*—and the threat of erasure. They'd tried to scare him into submission, to force him back into the box he'd spent his life escaping. But he wasn't that person anymore. He'd faced bullies, betrayal, and now these enforcers of a reality he refused to accept. *Each time, he'd chosen his response. Each time, he'd shaped the outcome and felt even stronger.*

"Then I won't give them a choice," he said, his voice firm. "If they want me, they'll have to deal with *what I become.*"

Elias's smile widened, a rare warmth breaking through his usual stoicism. "Good. Because the real fight is just beginning."

The hum returned—a low, menacing pulse vibrating through the alley. Shadows shifted along the walls, stretching unnaturally. Ray's heart quickened, but he didn't flinch. He turned toward the sound, squaring his shoulders, his mind already racing with possibilities. Whatever came next, he'd face it on his terms.

The city loomed around him, alive and unpredictable, a canvas he'd claimed as his own. He didn't know the full scope of the "framework" Elias spoke of, or who these enforcers truly were. But he didn't need to. Not yet. All he needed was the certainty burning within him: he was no longer a pawn in someone else's game.

He was the player.

And this reckoning was only the start.

Chapter - 19
The Final Conflict

"Fate whispers to the warrior, 'You cannot with stand the storm.' The warrior whispers back, 'I am the storm."

— Unknown

The alley stretched before Ray like a vein running through the city's underbelly, its damp walls glistening faintly under the stuttering glow of a distant streetlamp. His breath curled into the frigid night air, each exhale a testament to his defiance, his survival. His hands, still trembling from the leap and the fall that should have ended him, clenched into fists at his sides. The ache in his ribs pulsed with every beat of his heart, but his mind—his mind was a blade, sharp and unyielding. He had made his choice. There was no turning back.

Elias stood a few paces ahead, his silhouette framed against the shifting shadows, his silver hair catching the faint light like a beacon. His presence was steady, grounding, yet laced with an urgency Ray hadn't seen before. "They won't stop," Elias said, his voice cutting through the silence like a low wind across a barren plain. "You've seen too much. They will come for you again."

Ray met his gaze, the fire in his chest flaring despite the cold biting at his skin. "Let them come," he said, his words ringing with a certainty that surprised even him. "I'm done running."

The air trembled—a low hum rising from the pavement, vibrating through Ray's boots and into his bones. The streetlights flickered, their yellow glow stuttering as if reality itself were faltering. Shadows along the alley walls twisted, stretching unnaturally, like ink bleeding across a page. Elias's eyes narrowed, his posture stiffening. "They're already here."

Ray turned, his pulse quickening, expecting the suited men from the rooftop—the enforcers who had tried to erase him. But what emerged from the darkness was something far worse. Figures cloaked in distortion shimmered into existence, their outlines warping as if the fabric of the world couldn't contain them. They weren't human—not anymore, if they ever had been. Their forms shifted, faces flickering between blank voids and jagged, unreadable features. Their presence pressed against Ray's senses, a cold weight that made the air feel thick and hostile.

"You were warned," one of them said, its voice a layered echo, as if spoken by a chorus trapped in a single throat. The sound clawed at Ray's mind, urging him to recoil, to surrender. But he planted his feet, his jaw tightening.

"And I chose to see the truth," he shot back, stepping forward into the space where fear should have held him back.

The lead figure cocked its head, its form rippling like a mirage. "Then you leave us with no choice."

The ground beneath Ray lurched, the alley stretching and bending as reality twisted around him. The city's hum faded, replaced by a deafening silence that swallowed sound and sense alike. He stumbled, his vision blurring as the world dissolved into a void—neither here nor there, a space that existed between everything and nothing. His stomach flipped, the sensation of falling gripping him again, but this time there was no pavement below, no skyline above. Just endless, suffocating emptiness.

Elias moved first, a blur of motion cutting through the distortion. He struck with a force Ray couldn't comprehend, his fist connecting with the nearest entity and sending shockwaves rippling through the air. The figure staggered, its form fracturing like glass, only to reform an instant later. The others countered, shifting between states of existence—solid one moment, intangible the next. Ray's heart pounded as he realized the truth: physical strength wouldn't win this fight. These weren't beings he could punch or outrun. They were something else—guardians of a reality he'd dared to challenge.

Perception shapes reality. The thought anchored him, a lifeline in the chaos. Elias had taught him this. Every leap, every test, every moment of defiance had led to this. If he couldn't fight them with his hands, he'd fight them with his mind. Mind, the only thing he can always control no matter what the situation. Mind, the only thing on which no one can have control without his permission. And, he was determined to completely control his own mind and not let anyone or anything control it.

He closed his eyes, shutting out the swirling void, the flickering forms, the overwhelming urge to react. His breath slowed, deliberate, deep and steady, as he reached for the clarity he'd spent months cultivating. Fear clawed at the edges of his thoughts—fear of failure, of erasure, of losing everything he'd become—but he let it pass through him like wind through an open window. *Situations only have power if I let them,* he reminded himself. *I choose my response, I control them.*

When he opened his eyes, the distortions had slowed, their frenetic shifting stilled by an unseen force. The entities flickered, their outlines fraying as if struggling against a tide they couldn't see. Elias glanced at him, a grin breaking through the tension. "You're rewriting the space around you," he said, his voice steady amidst the chaos. "Good. Keep going."

Ray pushed harder, his focus narrowing to a single point. He didn't just want to survive this—he wanted to thrive, reclaim it. He envisioned stability, a world where the alley stood solid beneath his feet, where these beings held no sway. The air thickened, resisting his will at first, then bending to it. The void cracked, fissures of light splintering through the darkness like dawn breaking over a shattered horizon. The entities faltered, their forms unravelling, threads of their existence pulling apart.

"No!" one of them hissed, its voice fracturing as it lunged toward him. Ray didn't flinch. He held his ground, his mind an impenetrable fortress, picturing the city as it had been—alive, unbroken, his. The figure dissolved mid-step, its essence sucked into the void like smoke scattering in a storm. One by one, the others followed, their resistance crumbling against the weight of Ray's belief.

Silence crashed back into place, heavy and sudden. The alley reformed around him, its damp walls and flickering streetlamp snapping into focus as if nothing had happened. The city's hum returned, a distant heartbeat pulsing through the night. Ray's knees buckled, exhaustion slamming into him, but he caught himself against the wall, his breath ragged but triumphant.

Elias dusted off his coat, exhaling a sharp breath. "That was impressive."

Ray steadied himself, wiping sweat from his brow. "I don't think they're gone for good."

Elias nodded, his gaze drifting to the shadows. "No. But you're ready for them now."

Ray looked down at his hands, still trembling but alive with a power he could finally feel. He wasn't the lost boy who'd stood on rooftops searching for meaning. He wasn't the observer letting life happen to him. He had found it—within himself, in the choices he made, in the reality he shaped. "So, what now?" he asked, his voice steady despite the ache in his bones.

Elias's smile was faint but genuine. "Now, you decide what to do with your power."

Ray turned toward the city, its lights stretching out like a promise. The fight wasn't over—Elias was right; they'd come again. But that didn't scare him anymore. Not surprisingly, he was ready. Not just to survive, but to thrive and create. To push beyond the boundaries, they'd set for him. To be the storm they couldn't withstand. To help others see what he had seen. His purpose of life had transcended beyond him, it now had encompassed the entire humanity.

The hum returned, softer this time, a whisper at the edge of his senses. Ray straightened, his mind racing with possibilities. He thought of Leila, waiting at the café, oblivious to the battle he'd just fought. He thought of the mentorship program, the lives he'd touched, the movement his words had sparked. He'd built something real, something worth defending. And now, he understood: this wasn't just about him anymore. It was about everyone who'd dared to believe with him. It was the collective consciousness which was making him stronger and stronger. The more lives he meaningfully touched, the stronger he became.

"Let's go," he said, stepping past Elias toward the alley's mouth. The older man fell into step beside him, silent but present. The city loomed ahead, its towers and streets a canvas Ray had claimed as his own. He didn't know the full scope of the "they" Elias spoke of—the enforcers, the guardians of this framework—but he didn't need to. Not yet. Knowledge would come. For now, he had his resolve, his power, and the will to shape what lay ahead.

As they walked, the note from earlier flashed in his mind: *They are watching.* But now he wasn't worried about it, not any more. Let them watch, he thought. Infact, he wanted to let them see what he'd become. He wasn't a glitch to be erased or a variable to be controlled. He was Ray Carter—writer, fighter, creator—and he'd rewrite their rules if he had to.

The alley opened onto a bustling street, the city's pulse quickening around him. People moved past, their lives intersecting with his in ways he could only guess at. He paused, taking it all in—the noise, the light, the chaos of it all. This was his world now, not theirs. And he'd fight for it, not with fists or fear, but with the *one weapon only he could control*, the one they couldn't take: *his mind.*

Elias's voice broke his reverie. "You're quiet. What's on your mind?"

Ray exhaled, a faint smile tugging at his lips. "Everything. And nothing. I just… I know I can do this. Whatever comes next."

Elias clapped a hand on his shoulder, the gesture warm and solid. "You always could. You just had to see it."

Ray nodded, the weight of those words was very assuring and were settling over him like an impenetrable and inseparable armour. He'd leapt into the unknown before—off rooftops, through doors, into battles he didn't fully understand—and survived every time. *Not by luck, but by choice. By belief.* This final conflict wasn't the end; it was a beginning. A declaration that he wouldn't be contained, not by fear, not by enforcers, not by a reality someone else had written. *He will choose what he will become.*

The hum faded into the background, a distant echo of a threat he'd face again. But for now, the night was his. He stepped forward, the city unfolding before him, alive with possibility. He didn't know at all what the tomorrow held—what new shadows would rise, what truths he'd uncover—but he knew one thing: he'd meet it on his terms. *It will be his choice.*

And that was enough.

Chapter - 20
The Resolution

"The only limits that exist are the ones you place on yourself. It doesn't matter whether you think you can or cannot, you are generally right."

— **Unknown**

The city sprawled beneath Ray like a living tapestry, its lights pulsing with a rhythm that echoed the heartbeat of countless lives intertwined with his own. He stood at the rooftop's edge, the cold night air biting at his skin, carrying with it the faint tang of metal and exhaust. His jacket fluttered in the wind, a worn relic of the life he'd left behind, now a symbol of the battles he'd fought—and won. Elias stood beside him, his silver hair glinting in the dim glow of the skyline, his presence steady but silent, a guide who had become more than a teacher. The weight of the moment pressed against Ray's chest, not as a burden, but as a quiet, unshakable certainty.

He inhaled deeply, letting the crisp air fill his lungs, grounding him in the reality he'd reclaimed. Below, the streets churned with motion—cars weaving through arteries of asphalt, pedestrians hurrying toward destinations unknown. It was a world he'd once feared would swallow him whole, a labyrinth of meaninglessness he'd wandered aimlessly. But now, it was different. Not because the city had changed, but because he had. He saw it for what it truly was: a canvas, vast and unyielding, waiting for him to paint it with his choices.

Elias broke the silence, his voice low but resonant. "You understand now, don't you?"

Ray turned to him, meeting those sharp, knowing eyes. The question hung between them, heavy with the weight of everything they'd endured—the rooftop leaps, the shifting realities, the enforcers who'd sought to erase him. He nodded slowly, feeling the truth settle into his bones.

"Reality isn't something we just exist in. It's something we create, by choice, and we pay the price of our choice no matter what it is. Not choosing anything is also a choice, and we pay the price for that too."

A faint smile tugged at Elias's lips, the kind that carried both pride and a trace of melancholy. "And now, the choice is truly yours."

Ray's gaze drifted back to the city, the words sinking in. Choice. It had always been about choice. Not fate, not destiny, not some prewritten script handed down by unseen hands. He'd spent years believing he was a pawn, powerless against the currents of life. But Elias had shown him otherwise—shown him that the mind was a forge, perception the hammer, and every moment is a choice, a chance to shape what came next. The enforcers, those shadowy guardians of a controlled reality, had tried to strip that power from him. They'd failed. Not because he was stronger in body, but because *he'd chosen to refused to accept the limits set by them, chosen to refuse to let their version of the world define his.*

A New Dawn

The horizon glowed faintly, a sliver of dawn creeping into the bruised night sky. For Ray, it wasn't just the promise of a new day—it was the dawn of something greater, something he'd built with every choice, every step, every refusal to surrender. The fear that had once anchored him was gone, replaced by a fire that burned steady and bright. He had faced the void, leapt into it, and emerged not just alive but transformed to thrive, not just survive.

"They'll come again," Elias said, his tone a quiet warning as he followed Ray's gaze. "They always do. *The world resists those who refuse to be controlled.*"

Ray's jaw tightened, but his voice remained firm. "Let them come. This time, I decide who I am."

The words carried a weight he hadn't anticipated, a declaration that rippled through the air like a stone dropped into still water. He wasn't the Ray Carter who'd stood on rooftops contemplating nothingness, nor the one who'd let doubt dictate his steps. He was something new—a creator, a force, a man who understood that boundaries are to be pushed, limits were illusions he'd once placed on himself. The enforcers could return, their distorted forms and hollow threats could loom once more, but they'd find him ready. *Not reacting, but choosing.*

Elias clapped a hand on his shoulder, the gesture solid and warm. "You've taken the reins, Ray. Not just of your life, but of something bigger. It's not just about you Ray. What you do with it now—that's the real test."

Ray nodded, the responsibility was settling over him like a mantle and he was ready for that. He thought of the note from months ago—*They are watching*—and the later warning: *You've gone too far. Turn back.* Each had been a chain meant to bind him, a plea to retreat into the predictable, the safe. But safety was a cage, and he'd shattered its bars. He'd written his own response—*You can't stop what's already begun*—and left it for them to find, a gauntlet thrown at their feet. Let them watch. Let them see what he'd become.

Leaving The Past Behind

He turned from the rooftop's edge, descending the familiar stairwell with Elias at his side. The echoes of his boots against the concrete reverberated like a drumbeat, a rhythm of resolve. The city welcomed him as he stepped onto the street, its hum wrapping around him like an old friend. He walked with purpose, past the alley where he'd landed after his leap, past the shadows that had once held menace. They held no power now—not unless he gave it to them. He was in total control of his mind and the choice he was making.

Leila was waiting at the café, the place where so many threads of his journey had converged. The bell above the door chimed as he entered, a soft sound that felt like a homecoming. She sat at their usual table, a cup of coffee cradled in her hands, her curly hair spilling over her shoulders. She looked up as he approached, her sharp brown eyes narrowing with curiosity.

"You look… different," she said, tilting her head as if trying to puzzle him out.

Ray slid into the chair across from her, a smirk tugging at his lips. "I feel different."

She studied him, searching for something—an explanation, a crack in the calm he carried. "What happened up there?"

He leaned back, letting the warmth of the café seep into him. How could he explain it? The battle with the enforcers, the distortion of reality, the moment he'd seized control and reshaped the outcome? Words felt too small, too fragile to carry the weight of it. Some truths weren't meant to be spoken—in order to be completely understood, they were meant to be lived, to be experienced.

"I made a choice," he summarized the experience in four words, meeting her gaze. "And I'm not going back." He declared the outcome.

Leila arched an eyebrow, a smile tugging at the corner of her mouth. "Cryptic as ever. But I'll take it. You're still here, so I'm guessing you won whatever fight you were picking."

He chuckled, the sound light and free. "Something like that."

She didn't press further, and he was grateful for it. Leila had always known when to push and when to let him breathe. She'd been his anchor through the chaos, the one who'd pulled him from the ledge—literally and figuratively. Now, she was part of this new dawn, a witness to the man he was becoming.

The Road Ahead

The coffee steamed between them, its rich scent mingling with the quiet hum of conversation from other tables. Ray's mind drifted to the future—not as a distant, unreachable thing, but as a path unfolding with every step he took, like a mountain road unfolding after every new turn. He didn't need a prophecy or a map to guide him. *He'd learned the greatest truth of all: there was no singular destiny, no fate etched in stone. There was only the direction he chose, the reality he shaped, and the impact he left behind.*

His book had sparked a movement, its words igniting fires in hearts across the world. People wrote to him—strangers who'd found hope in his journey, who'd begun to see their own power to create. The mentorship program had grown, a community of seekers and builders who refused to let life happen to them. He'd become a voice, a catalyst, but he knew it wasn't about him alone. It was about what they could do together—a collective awakening of the collective consciousness, to the idea that reality bends to the intensity and type of belief. The reality is our choosing, consciously or unconsciously.

"They're still out there," he said after a moment, his voice low but steady. "The ones who tried to stop me."

Leila's expression sharpened, but she didn't flinch. "And?"

"And I'm not afraid of them, not anymore." He took a sip of his coffee, the bitterness grounding him. "They can watch me all they want. They can't touch what I've built unless I let them."

She nodded, a spark of pride in her eyes. "Good. Because I'd hate to have to drag you out of another existential spiral."

He laughed, the sound echoing through the café. "No more spirals. I promise."

The conversation shifted to lighter things—her latest project, his upcoming talks—but beneath it all, Ray felt the quiet pulse of purpose. He didn't know what form the enforcers would take next, or how they'd try to pull him back into their framework. But it didn't matter. He'd faced them once, reshaped their reality with his own, and he'd do it again if he had to.

A Quiet Certainty

As the night deepened, Ray stepped outside, the city wrapping around him like a cloak. The air was cold, but it no longer felt hostile. He tilted his head back, searching the sky for stars, finding only the faint glow of urban light. It didn't bother him. The stars were there, hidden but real, just like the truths he'd uncovered.

Elias's final words lingered in his mind: *The choice is truly yours.* And it was. Every moment, every breath, was a chance to decide who he'd become, what he'd create. The enforcers might return, their warnings might grow louder, but they'd lost their hold over him. He wasn't a glitch to be corrected or a threat to be contained or erased. He was Ray Carter—writer, fighter, shaper of his world— and he'd build a future they couldn't touch, not anymore.

He thought of the note he'd left on his desk, his defiance scrawled in ink: *You can't stop what's already begun.* It wasn't just bravado—it was a promise. To himself, to Leila, to everyone who'd found strength in his words.

The movement he'd sparked was bigger than him now, a tide of change that would roll on whether he stood at its helm or not.

Footsteps approached, and he turned to see Leila stepping out, her jacket pulled tight against the chill. "You're brooding again," she teased, nudging him with her elbow.

"Not brooding," he said, grinning. "Planning."

"For what?"

He looked out at the city, its lights stretching into the distance like a sea of possibility. "For whatever comes next."

She followed his gaze, a quiet understanding passing between them. "Well, whatever it is, you're not doing it alone." It was not a request, it was a decisive declaration.

The words warmed him more than the coffee ever could. He wasn't alone—not anymore. He had Leila, Elias, the countless lives he'd touched. Together, they'd face the shadows, the enforcers, the unknown. Together, they'd build something impregnable, something unstoppable.

Ray stepped forward, the pavement solid beneath his feet, the night alive with potential. This wasn't the end of his story—it was the beginning of something greater. A resolution not of closure, but of continuation. He'd rewritten his reality once, and he'd keep rewriting it, not just for himself, but for everyone who dared to believe with him. He would remain a work in progress, for ever.

The city hummed, a quiet symphony of choice and creation. Ray smiled into the darkness, unafraid.

This was only the start.

Epilogue
The Legacy

"The future belongs to those who believe in the beauty of their dreams."

— Eleanor Roosevelt

The café hummed with a quiet, resonant energy, its wooden floors creaking softly under the weight of footsteps and whispered conversations, a symphony of memory and possibility woven into its weathered grain. Ray Carter sat by the window, bathed in the soft, golden light of late afternoon, the sun's rays threading through the glass to cast faint, shifting shadows across the worn table before him. His hair, once a chaotic mess of black, was now streaked with silver, a testament to the decades that had slipped through his fingers since that first, fateful night on the rooftop. His journal lay open on the table, its pages a tapestry of ink—some scrawled in the haste of revelation, others etched with the careful deliberation of a man who'd learned to weigh his words. The world outside churned with life, a cacophony of horns, voices, and the ceaseless hum of 2065's advanced machinery threading through the city's veins, but here, in this small sanctuary, nothing seems to have changed, the time felt suspended… as if it was frozen—a pause between the echoes of what had been and the unwritten promise of what could still be.

He sipped his coffee, the familiar bitterness grounding him as it rolled over his tongue, a ritual that tethered him to the present while his mind drifted across the years. The cup trembled slightly in his hands—not from weakness, though age had begun to etch its lines into his bones, but from the weight of realization that pressed against his chest. It had been over twenty-two years since Elias had handed him that key, since the old man's cryptic words and the rusted rooftop door had unravelled the fabric of his reality. Back then, he'd been a boy lost in his own shadows, a nineteen-year-old drowning in apathy, convinced the world was a cage he'd never escape. He'd stood on rooftops not to leap into life, but to flirt with its absence, to test whether anything mattered enough to pull him back. Leila had been that pull—her stubborn faith in him, her refusal to let him fade, come what may. And Elias—Elias had been the spark, the friend, philosopher and guide who'd shown him the truth: the world wasn't a prison; it was a canvas, and he held the brush and each moment a choice, choice to choose what he wants his canvas to look like.

Now, at forty-two, Ray was something else entirely—a man who'd not only broken free from that cage but had spent his life showing others they could do the same. His dark eyes, once dulled by doubt, glowed with a quiet fire as he watched the faces passing beyond the window— each one a story, *a fragment of tomorrow waiting to unfold*. The city had evolved in those two decades, its skyline was sharper, its streets were alive with neural-linked drones and holographic billboards that whispered tailored promises to every mind they scanned. Technology had surged forward, weaving itself into the fabric of daily life, but beneath the shimmering surface, humanity lingered in the same dance of ambition and uncertainty Ray had known in 2042. Dreams were still postponed for practicality, passions still traded for stability—yet something had shifted. A ripple had begun, small at first, born of the words he'd scrawled in that journal, now that ripple was a tide sweeping across continents changing billions.

The café door chimed, a soft, familiar sound that pulled him from his reverie. A young boy stepped inside, no older than twelve, his dark eyes wide with a blend of curiosity and hesitation that Ray recognized like an old friend. His clothes hung slightly too big on his wiry frame—hand-me-downs, perhaps—his sneakers scuffed and patched from adventures that had worn them thin. In his hands, he clutched a battered copy of Ray's book, *Fragments of Tomorrow*, its cover creased and dog-eared from countless readings, its edges curling like a relic carried through a storm. The boy scanned the room, his gaze sweeping past the scattered patrons—a woman tapping at a neural tablet, a man murmuring into a holographic communication device—before landing on Ray. Their eyes locked, and for a moment, time folded in on itself. Ray saw himself in that boy—the uncertainty, the quiet hunger for something more, the spark waiting to ignite.

Ray smiled faintly, a knowing tug at the corner of his mouth as he set his cup down. He'd seen that look before—in his own reflection decades ago, in Leila's fierce optimism, in the countless faces that had crossed his path seeking meaning. The boy approached, his steps tentative but deliberate, the book held like a shield and a lifeline all at once. He stopped at the table, shifting his weight from one foot to the other, and when he spoke, his voice was soft but steady, carrying a resolve that belied his years.

"You're him, aren't you?" he asked, his eyes narrowing slightly as if testing the truth of his own words. "Ray Carter?"

Ray leaned back in his chair, the wood creaking under his weight, and nodded. "That's me. What's your name, kid?"

"Jaden," the boy replied, his grip tightening on the book as he straightened a little. "I… I heard about you. From my sister. She said your book changed her life—got her out of a bad place, made her start her own shop. I wanted to see if it was true—if you're really who they say you are."

Ray's smile widened, warmth spreading through his chest like sunlight breaking through clouds. He gestured to the chair across from him. "They say a lot of things, Jaden. Who do they say I am?"

Jaden hesitated, then slid into the seat, placing the book on the table as if it were an offering at an altar. "Someone who figured out how to make life matter, create the meaning of life," he said, his voice gaining strength with each word. "Someone who says we can choose what it all means—that we don't have to just… take what we're given."

Ray chuckled, the sound low and rich, echoing with years of lessons learned and battles won. "They're not wrong about that. Sit down, Jaden. Tell me why you're here— what brought you to this dusty old café looking for me."

The boy settled into the chair, his fingers tracing the book's worn spine as if drawing courage from its pages. "I don't know if my life matters," he said, his voice dropping to a near-whisper, raw with a vulnerability that cut through the café's quiet hum. "Everything feels so big—school, my parents, the city. It's like I'm just… me, and that's not enough. I want to understand how you did it—how you made your life mean something when it felt like nothing."

Ray leaned forward, resting his elbows on the table, his gaze steady and kind, piercing through the years to the boy he'd once been. "You're already on your way, you know that?" he said, his tone firm but gentle and assuring, a lifeline tossed across a stormy sea. "The fact that you're asking—that you walked in here, book in hand, looking for answers—it means you're not just existing. You're searching. That's where it starts, Jaden. That's where I started, that's where everyone started."

Jaden frowned, his fingers pausing on the book as he processed the words. "But how do you know what to do? What if I mess it up? My dad says I need to focus on school, get a good job, stop daydreaming about stuff that won't happen. What if he's right, and I try, and it all falls apart?"

Ray exhaled, his mind drifting back to the rooftops, the alleys, the moments of doubt and defiance that had carved him into the man he was now. He saw himself at nineteen, staring at a cracked ceiling, dismissing dreams as luxuries he couldn't afford. He saw the night Leila had found him, her half-eaten chocolate bar a quiet rebellion against his despair. He saw Elias, silver hair glinting under a streetlamp, handing him a key and a truth that had burned away the fog. "You will mess it up," he said, his voice steady with the weight of experience. "I did. Plenty of times—missed chances, wrong turns, nights I thought I'd lost everything. But here's the thing: *life isn't about getting it right every time. It's about choosing what you focus on—about deciding who you become through the mess.* The world doesn't have power over you unless you let it."

Jaden's brow furrowed, his young mind wrestling with the idea, a spark of understanding flickering in his dark eyes. "Like what you wrote about perception?" he asked, tapping the book's cover. "How what you think changes everything?"

"Exactly," Ray said, tapping the table for emphasis, the wood thudding softly under his finger. "What you believe, what you dwell on—it shapes your reality. Not because it's magic or some fairy tale, but because it changes how you see the world, how you respond to it, how you make your choices. And your response? That's your power, that's where the magic lies. I used to think life was a script I had to follow—school, job, settle down, repeat. I expected nothing, so I got nothing. Then I started expecting more, choosing more, and the world shifted with me."

Jaden nodded slowly, the spark catching, growing into a faint ember of possibility. Ray saw it—the same fire that had once flickered in him, fanned by Leila's stubborn faith and Elias's cryptic wisdom. He'd seen it in others too: in Kai's ink-stained hands, in Lena's trembling voice, in Tariq's relentless coding. Each had been a mirror, reflecting back the truth he'd fought to claim: a meaningful life wasn't about length or wealth—it was about impact, about giving others the tools to shape their own tomorrows.

The café door chimed again, and Ray glanced up as Leila stepped inside, her presence as vibrant as it had been two decades ago despite the grey streaking her curly hair. Her sharp brown eyes scanned the room, landing on Ray and Jaden with a knowing grin that softened the lines etched into her face by time and trials. She pulled up a chair without waiting for an invitation, settling in with the ease of someone who'd walked this path beside him from the beginning.

"Making new friends, I see," she said, her tone teasing but warm as she leaned back, crossing her arms. Her jacket, patched and weathered like Ray's, carried the same unspoken history—a testament to the storms they'd weathered together.

"Always," Ray replied, his voice light but his eyes glowing with gratitude. "This is Jaden. He's figuring out how to make his life matter."

Leila's grin softened into something gentler, more heartfelt, as she turned to the boy. "Good. That's the best place to start." She leaned in conspiratorially, her voice dropping to a playful whisper. "Let me tell you a secret about this guy—he didn't always have it figured out. Took me dragging him off a rooftop to get him moving."

Jaden's eyes widened, darting to Ray with a mix of awe and skepticism. "Is that true?"

Ray laughed, the sound echoing through the café with a richness born of decades of shared moments. Ray leaned forward towards Jaden and said, "Every word. She saved me before I even knew I needed saving—gave me a chocolate bar and a reason to step back from the edge.

Then, encouraged me to jump from the rooftop." Ray let out a hearty laughter again.

Leila waved a hand dismissively, though her eyes shone with pride. "You did the rest. Took that spark and turned it into a damn wildfire. Look at you now—still stirring up trouble, just in a better way."

Trouble. The word lingered, tugging at the edges of Ray's calm like a thread caught on a splinter. He thought of the envelope he'd received six months ago, slipped under his apartment door in the dead of night—no name, no address, just six words scrawled in sharp, precise letters: *You've gone too far. Turn back.* He'd held it in his hands, feeling the weight of their warning, their fear, the same cold precision he'd felt in that sterile prison decades ago. The enforcers—those shadowy architects of a controlled reality—hadn't vanished. They'd just retreated, regrouped, their presence a faint hum in the air, a ripple in the shadows when he least expected it. He'd taken out a pen and written his reply on the back: *You can't stop what's already begun.* Then he'd left it on his desk, knowing they'd find it—a gauntlet thrown, a line drawn in the sand.

They hadn't come for him immediately, but their warnings had grown sharper, more frequent. A month ago, a shadow had flickered outside his window—too deliberate, too angular to be a trick of light. A week later, a letter had arrived at a speaking event in Jakarta: *This ends when you do.* He'd burned it in the hotel sink, watching the flames consume their threat, the ashes curling into nothing. They could watch all they wanted;

they couldn't uproot what had taken hold. His belief was not a sapling anymore, it was a grand banyan tree which firmly ground and was going to withstand any storm. Like the roots of the banyan tree which grow from branches and go deep into ground, his movement had grown beyond him, a global tide of awakening—students in Mumbai staging walkouts inspired by his words, artists in São Paulo painting murals of shattered cages, coders in Seoul building neural networks to spread his message faster than their firewalls could block it.

"Trouble's not so bad," Ray said after a moment, his voice steady with a quiet defiance that hadn't dimmed with age. "Keeps things interesting."

Leila smirked, catching the undercurrent in his tone, her eyes glinting with the same fire that had pulled him from the ledge all those years ago. "You're not wrong. So, Jaden, what's your next step?"

The boy straightened, a newfound resolve tightening his jaw as he clutched the book tighter. "I want to write something," he said, his voice gaining strength with each syllable. "Not a book like this—not yet—but something mine. Something that says what I feel, what I see. My dad keeps telling me to focus on school, get a stable job, stop dreaming about stuff that won't happen. But I don't want to just… wait for life to start. I want to make it now."

Ray nodded, pride swelling in his chest like a tide rising to meet the shore. He saw it clearly now—Jaden wasn't just a kid with a book; he was a reflection of Ray's own beginning, a boy standing at the edge of possibility, teetering between doubt and daring. "Then do it," Ray said, his voice firm but kind, a command wrapped in encouragement. "Don't wait for permission or the perfect moment—those don't exist. Catch a moment and make it perfect. Start where you are, with what you have. Success doesn't come from having everything you need, it comes from making best of whatever you have. That's how it begins. I was like you once—staring at a ceiling, thinking nothing mattered, scared to try because I might fail. But failing's just part of it, Jaden. It's what you do after that counts. You are not defeated till you stop trying."

Jaden's eyes brightened, the ember flaring into a steady flame as he absorbed the words. "Thanks, Mr. Carter," he said, his grin breaking through the uncertainty like sunlight through a cracked wall. "I think… I think I can do this."

"You can," Ray replied, his tone unwavering. "And call me Ray. We're in this together now—part of the same story."

The boy beamed, the grin transforming his face as he stood, clutching the book like a talisman. "I'll come back," he promised, his voice ringing with determination. "When I've got something to show you—something real."

"I'll be here," Ray said, watching as Jaden slipped out into the evening, the door chiming behind him like a bell tolling the start of something new. He leaned back, the chair creaking under his weight, and let the moment settle over him—the quiet triumph of passing a torch, of seeing his legacy take root in a boy who'd walked the same shadowed path he once had. Humans are mortals but ideas are immortal, once passed on from generation to generation, they can live forever. Ray was feeling he would live on for ever, in form of his ideas.

Leila watched him, her grin softening into something deeper, more reflective. "Another one inspired," she said, crossing her arms with a mock sigh. "You're building quite the army, you know—writers, dreamers, troublemakers. Pretty soon, they'll be storming the streets with pens and ideas instead of guns."

Ray chuckled, but the weight of her words sank into him, rippling through the calm he carried. An army—not of fighters in the traditional sense, but of creators, seekers, people who'd learned to see beyond the limits imposed on them. His book, *Fragments of Tomorrow*, had been the spark—a bestseller that became a manifesto, its message echoing across continents: reality bends to belief, situations lose power when you don't react, and the mind is the ultimate tool of control, the choices decide the destiny, you always have a choice. From that single flame, new voices had risen—thinkers in Berlin crafting philosophies of choice, writers in Lagos weaving stories of resilience, leaders in Tokyo building communities that refused to bow to predictability. Workshops had turned into networks, networks into a global movement, its tendrils stretching further than Ray could have dreamed when he'd scribbled those first words in 2042.

It hadn't stopped with the book. The mentorship program he'd started in that crumbling community centre had grown into something vast—a constellation of hubs where people gathered to learn, to create, to challenge the framework that had once bound them. Students in Mumbai had staged walkouts, their banners quoting his lines: *"The world responds to what you expect."* Artists in São Paulo painted murals of shattered cages, their colours bleeding across grey concrete, a visual echo of his call to break free. Coders in Seoul built neural networks—open-source, defiant—spreading his message faster than the enforcers' firewalls could block it, their screens flashing his words in defiance of a world that demanded conformity. The tide had swelled beyond him, an awakening collective consciousness he'd ignited but no longer controlled, its momentum carrying it into places he'd never seen.

And yet, the enforcers remained—a constant, unyielding shadow at the edges of his life. Their presence was a hum he felt in quiet moments, a vibration threading through the air when the world grew too still. They hadn't vanished after that night in the alley, nor after the sterile prison where he'd shattered their reality with his own. They'd just retreated, regrouped, waiting for an opportune time, their warnings sharpening with every victory his movement claimed. Three months ago, a drone had hovered outside his window in the dead of night, its lens glinting like an eye—too precise, too deliberate to be random. A week later, a package had arrived at a workshop in Cape Town: a single sheet of paper, blank except for the words *This ends when you do*, written in that same sharp script he'd come to know too well. He'd burned it in a fire pit behind the venue, the flames curling the paper into ash as the attendees watched in silence, their faces set with a resolve that mirrored his own.

They could watch all they wanted—they couldn't stop what had taken hold. His legacy wasn't just his anymore; it was theirs, a tapestry woven by every hand that dared to pick up the thread. Jaden was just the latest, a boy whose story would join the countless others Ray had sparked into being. The enforcers had underestimated him once, thinking him to be just a glitch, they thought they could correct, or control, or contain or erase a single man and silence his voice. But that voice had multiplied many fold, resonating in hearts and minds across the globe, a chorus they couldn't mute with threats or shadows.

"An army of choice," Ray mused aloud, his gaze drifting to the city beyond the glass, where dusk painted the towers in hues of amber and steel. "That's what Elias wanted, isn't it?"

Leila nodded, her expression softening with a quiet reverence. "He'd be proud. Wherever he is."

Elias. The name carried a quiet ache, a thread Ray couldn't quite tie off despite the years. He'd vanished after that night in the alley, his final words—*Fight for the truth*—a whisper that echoed through every choice Ray had made since. He'd searched for him in the early years, haunting cafés and rooftops, peering into shadows for a glimpse of silver hair or a knowing smile. But Elias had slipped away like smoke, leaving only his lessons etched into Ray's bones. Had he been taken by the enforcers, erased like Mara, the partner he'd lost to their wrath? Had he chosen to step back, trusting Ray to carry the torch alone? The uncertainty lingered, a bittersweet note in the symphony of Ray's life, but he honoured it by living what

Elias had taught him: the world was theirs to shape, not to be shaped by.

The café grew quieter as dusk deepened, the last patrons drifting out into the evening, their voices fading into the city's hum. Ray flipped to a fresh page in his journal, his pen hovering over the paper, its tip trembling faintly with the weight of what he wanted to capture. He wrote:

The future isn't a gift bestowed on us—it's a garden we deliberately and carefully plant with every thought, every choice. I've spent my life learning to tend it, to show others they can too. The enforcers may watch, may threaten, but they can't uproot what's taken hold—not anymore. This legacy isn't mine alone; it's ours, a tapestry woven by everyone who dares to believe. Jaden's just the latest thread, one more spark in a fire that's spread too far to douse. There'll be more—countless more—and the dance doesn't end; it evolves. I don't know how long I've got left, but I know this: I've lived a life that matters, not in years, but in depth. That's enough.

He paused, glancing at Leila, her sharp eyes scanning the page over his shoulder. "Think it's enough?" he asked, his voice soft but steady.

She tilted her head, a faint smile tugging at her lips. "Enough for now. You've never been one to stop, though—always another page, another fight."

"True," he said, closing the journal with a soft thud that echoed through the quiet café. "There's always more to build—more to plant."

The hum returned then—faint, almost imperceptible, a vibration threading through the air like a whisper from the shadows. Ray stilled, his senses sharpening as the hairs on his neck prickled. Leila noticed it too, her eyes narrowing as she scanned the room, her hand resting lightly on the table, ready to move. The shadows along the walls shifted, stretching unnaturally, bending the light in ways that defied reason. For a moment, Ray saw them—silhouettes at the edge of his vision, their forms flickering like static on an old screen, their presence a cold weight pressing against the warmth of the café.

"They're back," Leila whispered, her voice tense but unshaken, her gaze darting to the corners where the shadows pooled.

Ray stood, his chair scraping against the floor with a sharp, deliberate sound that cut through the stillness. His heart thudded, a steady rhythm of defiance pulsing through him, but his mind was clear, honed by years of facing this very threat. "Let them come," he said, his voice a quiet thunder rolling through the space, unshaken by the weight of their intent.

The air thickened, the hum rising to a low roar that vibrated through the wooden beams and rattled the glass in the windows. The door didn't open—no chime sounded—but figures emerged from the shadows, their outlines warping the space around them like heat rising from asphalt. Not just two this time, nor the dozen he'd faced in the alley years ago, but a legion—a dozen, then two dozen, their forms multiplying as if summoned from the cracks in reality itself. Their faces flickered, blank voids one moment, jagged distortions the next, their presence a suffocating force that bent the café's edges into a blur. The remaining patrons froze, oblivious, trapped in a moment these enforcers controlled, their lives paused like a film on hold.

The lead figure stepped forward, its form more defined than the others, its voice a layered echo that clawed at Ray's mind like fingernails on glass. "You were warned, Mr. Carter," it said, each syllable a chorus of menace. "This ends now."

Ray squared his shoulders, his gaze unflinching as he stepped into the space where fear should have held him back. His hands no longer trembled; they were steady, forged by decades of choosing his response over their threats. "You don't get to decide that," he said, his words cutting through the chaos with a clarity that defied their distortion. Pointing his right hand index figure towards his chest Ray said, "I do."

The figure tilted its head, a flicker of uncertainty breaking its composure—a crack in the façade Ray had learned to exploit. He felt it then—their power wasn't absolute. They thrived on reaction, on fear, on doubt, on uncertainty, on the surrender of will. He wouldn't give them any of it—not now, not ever. He closed his eyes, shutting out their flickering forms, the warping walls, the overwhelming urge to recoil. His breath slowed, deliberate and steady, as he reached for the certainty he'd spent his life cultivating—the certainty that had carried him through leaps, through battles, through decades of defiance.

When he opened his eyes, the café steadied, its edges snapping back into focus as the distortions faltered. The figures wavered, their outlines fraying like threads caught in a gale, struggling against a force they couldn't grasp. Leila stood beside him, her presence a silent pillar, her sharp eyes glinting with the same fire that had saved him all those years ago. "You're rewriting it again," she said, her voice low but fierce, a grin tugging at her lips.

Ray pushed harder, his focus narrowing to a single, unshakable point. He didn't just want to survive this—he wanted to reclaim it, to reshape it, to prove that their framework held no dominion over him or the world he'd built. He envisioned the café as it had been—warm, solid, alive with the quiet hum of possibility. He envisioned the movement—Jaden's spark, the global tide of creators, the countless lives that had woven his legacy into something vast and unbreakable. The air resisted at first, a cold pressure pushing back, then bent to his will, yielding like clay under a sculptor's hands.

The figures lunged, their forms clawing through the thickening space, but the café cracked around them—light spilling through fissures in their reality, splintering their hold. They dissolved, pulled into the void they'd summoned, their echoes swallowed by a silence that crashed into place like a wave breaking on stone. The room snapped back into focus—the wooden floors steady, the lights glowing warm and constant, the hum gone. The frozen patrons blinked, resuming their conversations as if nothing had happened, oblivious to the battle that had unfolded in their midst.

Leila exhaled, her grin widening as she shook her head. "You're getting damn good at that."

Ray smirked, adrenaline still pulsing through him like a second heartbeat, his ribs aching but his spirit soaring. "Practice makes perfect," he said, brushing a bead of sweat from his brow. "Took me twenty years to figure out the trick."

She laughed, the sound bright and unburdened, cutting through the lingering tension. "Guess I'll stick around for the next twenty—see what else you pull off."

Ray stepped outside, the city wrapping around him like a cloak, it's cool air a balm against the heat of battle. Leila joined him, her jacket pulled tight against the evening chill, her presence a reminder of the strength they'd forged together through decades of storms and triumphs. The skyline stretched before them, sharper and taller than it had been in 2042, its towers piercing a sky now streaked with the first hints of dusk. Somewhere out there, Jaden was writing his story—scribbling his fears, his dreams, his defiance into something real. Others were waking up, too—choosing their paths, building their realities, adding their voices to the chorus that Ray had begun.

The enforcers would return—they always did, their warnings growing sharper with every ripple his movement sent through their framework. Ray didn't know how long he had left, how many more battles he'd face before age or their shadows claimed him. But it didn't matter. He'd lived a life that mattered—not in years, but in depth, in the lives he'd touched, the possibilities he'd awakened. His legacy wasn't a monument etched in stone; it was a living thing, living in the collective consciousness of people, a garden tended by countless hands, its roots too deep and too strong for the enforcers to uproot.

"So," Leila said, nudging him with her elbow as they stood shoulder to shoulder, "what happens now?"

Ray looked to the horizon, where the last light of day bled into the coming night, painting the city in hues of amber and steel. "Now, we build a world that belongs to us—all of us," he said, his voice steady with a quiet, unshakable certainty. "*One choice at a time.*"

He stepped forward, the pavement solid beneath his feet, the city unfolding around him like a promise he'd keep—not just for himself, but for Jaden, for Leila, for everyone who'd dared to believe with him. The hum was gone, the shadows still, but Ray knew they'd return. When they did, he'd be ready—not with fear, but with the power he'd claimed: belief. The dance didn't end; it evolved, and he'd lead it as long as he could, passing the torch to those who'd carry it further than he'd ever dreamed.

You are not defined by the storms you face but by the light you carry through them. Your kindness, resilience, and hope make you unbreakable, and even when the wind howl, your spirit whispers: "I will not be moved; I will rise stronger than ever."

The night stretched before him, alive with possibility—a canvas vast and unyielding, waiting for its next stroke. Ray smiled into the darkness, unafraid, his heart a steady drumbeat of purpose. This wasn't the end of his story; it was the beginning of something greater, a legacy that

www.ingramcontent.com/pod-product-compliance
Lightning Source LLC
LaVergne TN
LVHW052257210726
843527LV00040B/548